What's there to see?

Introduction	2
Contents	3
Features to look out for...	4-7
Timeline	8-9
Anglo-Saxon and Norman England, c 1060-1087 Student Book sample chapter	10-41
Writing Historically	42-43
Preparing for your exams	44-45
ActiveLearn Digital Service and Pearson Progression Services	46-47
Next steps	48

If you like what you see...
Order your **FREE** Evaluation Pack, which includes a copy of one of our Student Books!

www.pearsonschools.co.uk/FreeHistoryEvaluation16.

Features to look out for...

Throughout this sample chapter, you'll get a glimpse of all the features we have created to help all your students succeed in history.

Key Term
Unfamiliar and historically important words are defined for students.

Exam-style questions
Realistic exam-style questions appear in every chapter with short tips to help students get started with their answers – ideal for homework and assessments.

1.1 Anglo-Saxon society

Extend your knowledge
Thegns
Thegns were divided into king's thegns, who held their land direct from the king and served him directly, and those who held their land from earls and other thegns.

When a man became a thegn, he paid a tax called a heriot. Heriot meant 'war gear' and the tax required a thegn to equip himself with a helmet and coat of mail, a horse and harness, and a sword and spear.

Earls
Earls* were the most important aristocrats: the most important men in the country after the king. The relationship between the king and his earls was based on loyalty. The earls competed against each other to be the one the king trusted and relied on the most, so that the king would give them the greatest rewards and honour. Sometimes, earls even challenged the king to get more power.

Figure 1.2 The main earldoms of England in 1060.

Key term
Earls*
Highest Anglo-Saxon aristocracy. The word came from the Danish 'jarl' and meant a chieftain who ruled a region on behalf of the king. The area controlled by an earl is called an earldom.

Changing social status
In other parts of Europe, such as in Normandy, people's status in society depended on ancestry: the importance of their family and ancestors. Anglo-Saxon society was much less rigid than this.

- A peasant who prospered and obtained five hides of land that he paid tax on could gain the status of a thegn.
- Merchants who made a number of trips abroad in their own ships could also become thegns.
- Slaves could be freed by their masters – and free peasants could sell themselves into slavery as a desperate measure to feed their families.
- At the top of the social system, thegns could be raised to the status of earls (and earls could be demoted to thegns). Earls could sometimes even become kings.

Exam-style question, Section B
Describe **two** features of the social system of Anglo-Saxon England. **4 marks**

Exam tip
This question is about identifying key features. You need to identify two relevant points and then develop each point. For example: 'The social system was not fixed. This meant a free peasant who did very well could become a thegn.'

Extend your knowledge
Anglo-Saxon England
The areas of Britain controlled by Anglo-Saxons had changed over the centuries. Viking invasions had taken control of vast areas, which had then been recaptured. Anglo-Saxon England also had hostile neighbours: Wales, Scotland and Ireland and, to the south, Normandy. The location of Normandy is included on this map, but it was never under Anglo-Saxon control.

The power of the English monarchy
In 1060, the king (monarch) was Edward the Confessor. He was the most powerful person in Anglo-Saxon England. He governed the country.

Powers of the king
- **Law-making:** the king created new laws and made sure they were enforced throughout the country.
- **Money:** the king controlled the production of the silver pennies used as money.
- **Landownership:** the king owned large estates and could grant land out to his followers. He could also take land away from those who had acted against him.
- **Military power:** the king had the ability to raise a national army and fleet.
- **Taxation:** the king decided when taxes should be paid and a national taxation system delivered this tax to him.

Duties of the people
- To obey the law as it was passed down through the king's local representatives.
- To use the king's coins. Forging coins was a very serious crime.
- Land carried with it obligations to the king. The main two obligations were payment of tax and military service.
- Landholders had to provide and equip fighters for the army or fleet; otherwise they were fined or lost their land.
- Landholders had to pay their taxes, otherwise they were fined or lost their land.

Figure 1.3 The powers of Edward the Confessor and the duties of his people. The image in the middle is a representation of Edward's royal seal. This was attached to his royal orders to show they came from the king.

The king's role was to protect his people from attack and give them laws to maintain safety and security at home. In return, the people of England owed him service. Every boy swore an oath* when they reached 12 years of age to be faithful to the king. The oath was administered by the shire reeve* at a special ceremony held each year (see Source A).

Source A
The oath sworn by Anglo-Saxon boys once they reached 12 years of age.

All shall swear in the name of the Lord, before whom every holy thing is holy, that they will be faithful to the king... From the day on which this oath shall be rendered, no one shall conceal the breach of it on the part of a brother or family relation, any more than in a stranger.

How powerful was Edward the Confessor?
Kings of Anglo-Saxon England held their power ultimately because they led armies. Anglo-Saxon kings had clawed England back from Viking control. Edward the Confessor was not a warrior king, but his earls and their thegns were a powerful military force and he relied on his earls, especially Earl Godwin, to protect England from attack.

Kings who were war leaders gained legitimacy for their rule because they could hand out the wealth and land of their defeated enemies to their followers. When kings did not have success in battle then their power could be reduced. However, Edward had other reasons that made him a legitimate king.

Key terms
Oath*
A solemn promise to do something. Anglo-Saxons swore oaths on holy relics to make them especially binding. A relic was often a body part of a dead saint, kept in a special casket.

Shire reeve*
An official of the king: his sheriff. Sheriffs managed the king's estates, collected revenue for him and were in charge of local courts.

Extend your knowledge
Extra details to deepen students' knowledge and understanding.

Sources
A wide variety of contemporary sources help bring the subject to life, and give important insight into each period.

1.2 The last years of Edward the Confessor and the succession crisis

Source B

The death of Edward the Confessor, portrayed in the Bayeux Tapestry.

Activity

KWL is a strategy to help you take control of your own learning. It stands for Know – Want to know – Learned. This is how it works:

a Draw a table with three columns: 'Know', 'Want to know', 'Learned'.
b For any topic you are learning about, write down what you know about it already.
c Next, write down what else you'd like know, what questions you have about what you know.
d When you find out the answers, write them in the 'Learned' column.

Use this method to make notes on this section. Here's an example:

Know	Want to know	Learned
Tostig was from Wessex; Northumbria was different.	Why was Northumbria different?	Part of Northumbria in Danelaw. Different laws, different language, tax lower.

Summary

- The house of Godwin had become the real 'power behind the throne' in Anglo-Saxon England.
- Harold's embassy to Normandy and his decisions over Tostig had major consequences.
- Edward the Confessor died childless, causing a succession crisis.

Checkpoint

Strengthen

S1 When did: Harold become Earl of Wessex; Tostig get exiled; King Edward die?
S2 Describe two aspects of the house of Godwin that made them so powerful.

Challenge

C1 In your own words, summarise three reasons why you think Harold went against King Edward's wishes over the rising against Tostig.
C2 What else would it be useful to know about the consequences of Tostig's exile?

How confident do you feel about your answers to these questions? If you are not sure that you have answered them well, try the above study skills activity.

Activities

Engaging and accessible activities tailored to the skills focuses of each unit to support and stretch students' learning.

Summary

Bullet-point list of the key points from the material at the end of each chunk of learning – great for embedding the core knowledge and handy for revision.

Checkpoint

Students are asked to check and reflect on their learning regularly.

'**Strengthen**' sections help consolidate knowledge and understanding.

'**Challenge**' questions encourage evaluation and analysis of what's being studied.

Features to look out for...

At the end of each chapter, '**Recap**' spreads give students a chance to consolidate and reflect upon what they've learned. These sections include a recall quiz (ideal for a quick-fire knowledge check in class or revision aid), activities to help students summarise and analyse the chapter, and consider how it links to what they've learned throughout the course.

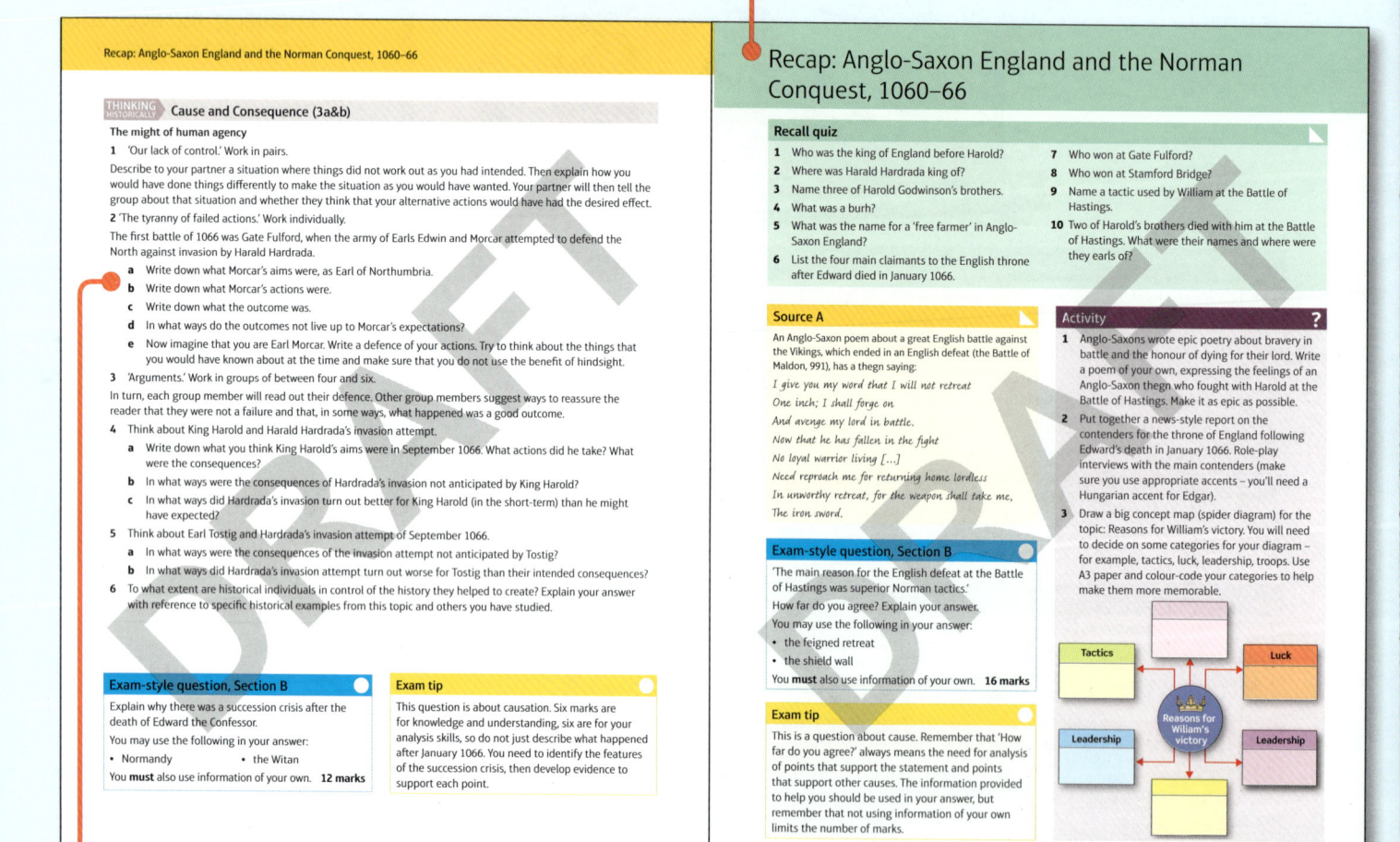

Recap: Anglo-Saxon England and the Norman Conquest, 1060–66

THINKING HISTORICALLY — Cause and Consequence (3a&b)

The might of human agency

1. 'Our lack of control.' Work in pairs.
   Describe to your partner a situation where things did not work out as you had intended. Then explain how you would have done things differently to make the situation as you would have wanted. Your partner will then tell the group about that situation and whether they think that your alternative actions would have had the desired effect.

2. 'The tyranny of failed actions.' Work individually.
   The first battle of 1066 was Gate Fulford, when the army of Earls Edwin and Morcar attempted to defend the North against invasion by Harald Hardrada.
   a. Write down what Morcar's aims were, as Earl of Northumbria.
   b. Write down what Morcar's actions were.
   c. Write down what the outcome was.
   d. In what ways do the outcomes not live up to Morcar's expectations?
   e. Now imagine that you are Earl Morcar. Write a defence of your actions. Try to think about the things that you would have known about at the time and make sure that you do not use the benefit of hindsight.

3. 'Arguments.' Work in groups of between four and six.
   In turn, each group member will read out their defence. Other group members suggest ways to reassure the reader that they were not a failure and that, in some ways, what happened was a good outcome.

4. Think about King Harold and Harald Hardrada's invasion attempt.
   a. Write down what you think King Harold's aims were in September 1066. What actions did he take? What were the consequences?
   b. In what ways were the consequences of Hardrada's invasion not anticipated by King Harold?
   c. In what ways did Hardrada's invasion turn out better for King Harold (in the short-term) than he might have expected?

5. Think about Earl Tostig and Hardrada's invasion attempt of September 1066.
   a. In what ways were the consequences of the invasion attempt not anticipated by Tostig?
   b. In what ways did Hardrada's invasion attempt turn out worse for Tostig than their intended consequences?

6. To what extent are historical individuals in control of the history they helped to create? Explain your answer with reference to specific historical examples from this topic and others you have studied.

Exam-style question, Section B

Explain why there was a succession crisis after the death of Edward the Confessor.
You may use the following in your answer:
• Normandy
• the Witan
You **must** also use information of your own. **12 marks**

Exam tip

This question is about causation. Six marks are for knowledge and understanding, six are for your analysis skills, so do not just describe what happened after January 1066. You need to identify the features of the succession crisis, then develop evidence to support each point.

Recap: Anglo-Saxon England and the Norman Conquest, 1060–66

Recall quiz

1. Who was the king of England before Harold?
2. Where was Harald Hardrada king of?
3. Name three of Harold Godwinson's brothers.
4. What was a burh?
5. What was the name for a 'free farmer' in Anglo-Saxon England?
6. List the four main claimants to the English throne after Edward died in January 1066.
7. Who won at Gate Fulford?
8. Who won at Stamford Bridge?
9. Name a tactic used by William at the Battle of Hastings.
10. Two of Harold's brothers died with him at the Battle of Hastings. What were their names and where were they earls of?

Source A

An Anglo-Saxon poem about a great English battle against the Vikings, which ended in an English defeat (the Battle of Maldon, 991), has a thegn saying:

I give you my word that I will not retreat
One inch; I shall forge on
And avenge my lord in battle.
Now that he has fallen in the fight
No loyal warrior living [...]
Need reproach me for returning home lordless
In unworthy retreat, for the weapon shall take me,
The iron sword.

Activity

1. Anglo-Saxons wrote epic poetry about bravery in battle and the honour of dying for their lord. Write a poem of your own, expressing the feelings of an Anglo-Saxon thegn who fought with Harold at the Battle of Hastings. Make it as epic as possible.

2. Put together a news-style report on the contenders for the throne of England following Edward's death in January 1066. Role-play interviews with the main contenders (make sure you use appropriate accents – you'll need a Hungarian accent for Edgar).

3. Draw a big concept map (spider diagram) for the topic: Reasons for William's victory. You will need to decide on some categories for your diagram – for example, tactics, luck, leadership, troops. Use A3 paper and colour-code your categories to help make them more memorable.

Exam-style question, Section B

'The main reason for the English defeat at the Battle of Hastings was superior Norman tactics.'
How far do you agree? Explain your answer.
You may use the following in your answer:
• the feigned retreat
• the shield wall
You **must** also use information of your own. **16 marks**

Exam tip

This is a question about cause. Remember that 'How far do you agree?' always means the need for analysis of points that support the statement and points that support other causes. The information provided to help you should be used in your answer, but remember that not using information of your own limits the number of marks.

Our Student Books include '**Thinking Historically**' activities that target four key strands of understanding: evidence, interpretations, causation & consequence and change & continuity.

These are all based on the '*Thinking Historically*' approach we've developed in conjunction with Dr Arthur Chapman at the Institute of Education, University College London.

This is what's in the **sample chapter**...

Contents

Timeline	6
Chapter 1 Anglo-Saxon England and the Norman Conquest, 1060-66	**8**
1.1 Anglo-Saxon society	9
1.2 The last years of Edwards the Confessor and the succession crisis	19
1.3 The rival claimants for the throne	25
1.4 The Norman invasion	31
Recap page	37
Writing Historically	38
Chapter 2 William I in power: securing the kingdom, 1066-87	**40**
2.1 Establishing control	41
2.2 The causes and outcomes of Anglo-Saxon resistance, 1068-71	47
2.3 The legacy of resistance to 1087	53
2.4 Revolt of the Earls, 1075	61
Recap page	65
Writing Historically	66

Chapter 3 Norman England, 1066-88	**68**
3.1 The feudal system and the Church	69
3.2 Norman government	77
3.3 The Norman aristocracy	83
3.4 William I and his sons	87
Recap page	91
Writing Historically	92
Anglo-Saxon and Norman England, c1060-88: Preparing for your exam	94
Answers	100
Index	101

And here's what you'll find in the **Student Book**...

Timeline: Anglo-Saxons and Normans

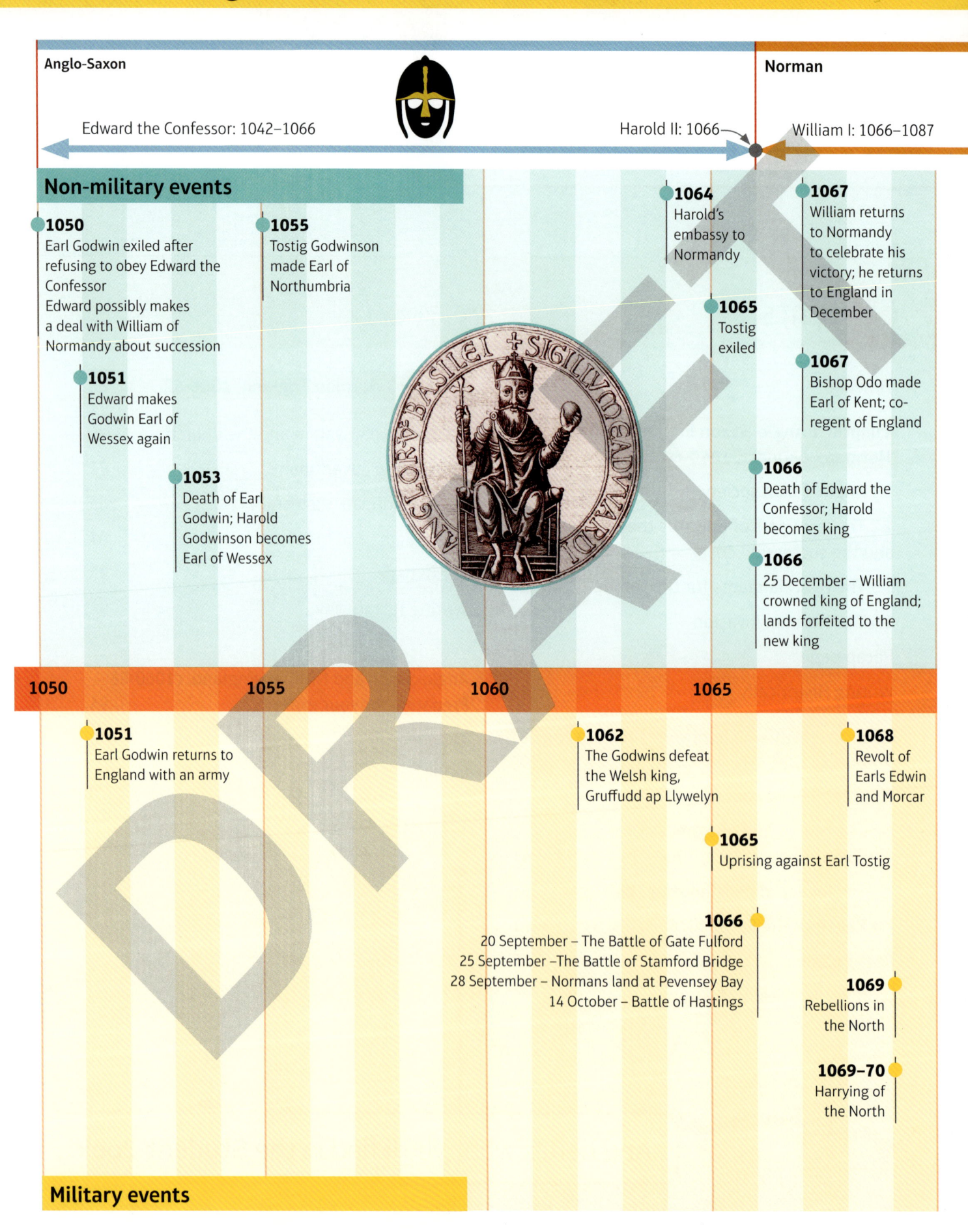

Anglo-Saxon | **Norman**

Edward the Confessor: 1042–1066 — Harold II: 1066 — William I: 1066–1087

Non-military events

1050 Earl Godwin exiled after refusing to obey Edward the Confessor
Edward possibly makes a deal with William of Normandy about succession

1051 Edward makes Godwin Earl of Wessex again

1053 Death of Earl Godwin; Harold Godwinson becomes Earl of Wessex

1055 Tostig Godwinson made Earl of Northumbria

1064 Harold's embassy to Normandy

1065 Tostig exiled

1066 Death of Edward the Confessor; Harold becomes king

1066 25 December – William crowned king of England; lands forfeited to the new king

1067 William returns to Normandy to celebrate his victory; he returns to England in December

1067 Bishop Odo made Earl of Kent; co-regent of England

1050 — 1055 — 1060 — 1065

Military events

1051 Earl Godwin returns to England with an army

1062 The Godwins defeat the Welsh king, Gruffudd ap Llywelyn

1065 Uprising against Earl Tostig

1066
20 September – The Battle of Gate Fulford
25 September – The Battle of Stamford Bridge
28 September – Normans land at Pevensey Bay
14 October – Battle of Hastings

1068 Revolt of Earls Edwin and Morcar

1069 Rebellions in the North

1069–70 Harrying of the North

William II (William Rufus): 1087–1100

1070 Stigand replaced by Lanfranc as Archbishop of Canterbury

1071 Edwin's lands forfeited

1076 Inquiry into Bishop Odo's illegal land grabs

1080 Robert and William reconciled

1082 Bishop Odo imprisoned

1083 Death of Matilda, William's wife and trusted regent

1084 Heavy geld tax levied

1085 William orders Domesday Book surveys

1086 First drafts of the Domesday Book shown to William; landholders summoned to swear allegiance

1087 Death of William in Normandy William II (William Rufus) crowned king of England

| 1070 | 1075 | 1080 | 1085 | 1090 |

1070–71 Hereward the Wake and the revolt at Ely

1075 Revolt of the Earls

1077 Robert Curthose rebels against his father, William

1085 Threat of Danish invasion means William brings thousands more troops into England

1088 Odo leads rebellion against William Rufus, which is defeated

9

Anglo-Saxon and Norman England, c 1060-1087, Student Book sample chapter

01 | Anglo-Saxon England and the Norman Conquest, 1060–66

By the time of King Edward the Confessor (1042–66), England had been Anglo-Saxon for 600 years. Through those centuries, England had developed a very strong government. It also had a prosperous economy, boosted by extensive trade links across the North Sea and the Channel. England was a Christian country, but Christian teachings were mixed with ancient beliefs about how people should behave. One key belief was that, in return for protection from a lord, his people owed him service. For example, in return for land to farm, a man would owe military service to his lord.

England had faced a terrible threat for centuries: the Vikings. These were Scandinavians who had raided settlements all along the coasts of Europe. In England, their raids were followed by invasions, so that many parts of northern England had Viking settlers. The kings before Edward had been Vikings: Cnut and his two sons. One of the reasons that England had a very well-organised government was because of the need for all Anglo-Saxons to work together to deal with the Vikings. The way Christian belief had developed was also connected to the threat of invasion. People understood Viking raids as punishment from God for the sins of the English people. The Church said that the only way to prevent further violence and invasion was through prayer and providing support for the Church.

Across the Channel, Viking settlers had taken control of Normandy (Norman meant 'North-man': Vikings from the north). By 1060, these Viking settlers had become very like their French neighbours, but they still had strong links with Scandinavia, allowing Viking raiders to take shelter in their harbours and ports. They also remained a powerful military threat.

Learning outcomes

In this chapter you will find out:
- how Anglo-Saxon society worked
- how Harold Godwinson became king of England
- why other people also claimed the throne of England
- what happened in 1066: the year of the Norman invasion.

1.1 Anglo-Saxon society

Learning outcomes

- Understand the Anglo-Saxon social system and the power of the monarch.
- Understand how England was governed and the role of the Church.
- Understand the economy of Anglo-Saxon England.

What was England like in 1060? Compared to now, there were very few people: about two million in the whole of England – less than half the population of London today. Life was hard and life expectancy was low: most people died in their thirties. Almost everyone farmed land in order to grow what they needed to live on, although right at the top of Anglo-Saxon* society were the aristocracy* – the social elite. Right at the bottom of Anglo-Saxon society were the slaves.

Key terms

Anglo-Saxon*

People who had settled in England after the Romans left Britain. They came from different parts of what is now Germany, Belgium and the Netherlands.

Aristocracy*

The people in society who are seen as being important because of their wealth and power, which they have often inherited from their parents and ancestors.

The social system
Peasant farmers

The majority of Anglo-Saxons were peasant farmers, who rented small farms that they worked for themselves and their families. Peasants did a set amount of work for the local lord as well as working the land to support themselves and their families. If they did not carry out this work for their lord then the peasants could lose their right to use the land.

There was also a group of peasants called ceorls* who were free to go and work for another lord if they wanted to. These ceorls still had to carry out some services for their local lord in return for the right to farm the land. No-one used land without carrying out some kind of service to someone else.

Key term

Ceorls*

'Free' peasant farmers not tied to their land.

Slaves

10% of the Anglo-Saxon population were slaves. Slaves could be bought and sold. If they committed crimes, they were often not punished as harshly as other people because it might damage their ability to work: they were seen more like property than people. The Normans thought that owning slaves was barbaric, but it was a normal part of Anglo-Saxon society.

Thegns

Thegns were the local lords. There were between 4,000 and 5,000 thegns by 1060. A thegn was an important man in the local community: holding more land than the peasants (more than five hides* of land), and living in a manor house with a tower and with a church. Thegns were the aristocracy of the Anglo-Saxon age, its warrior class.

Key term

Hides*

The measurement used for land in Anglo-Saxon and Norman England. One hide was about 120 acres: the amount a family needed to support themselves.

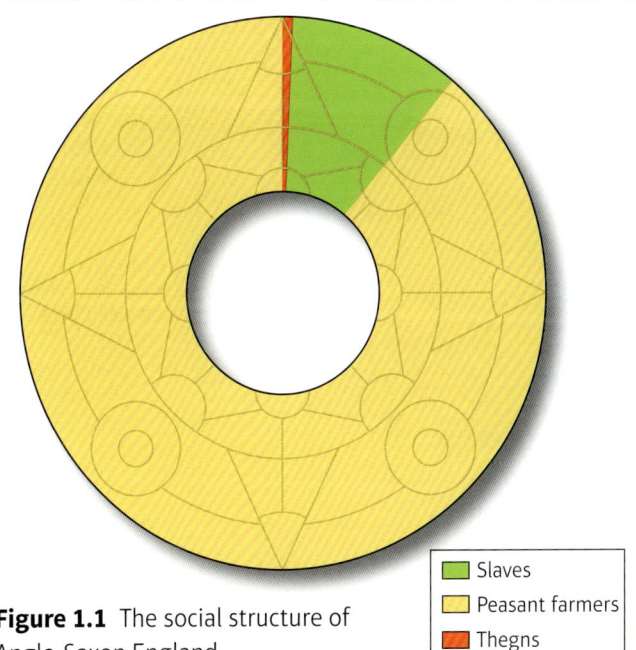

Figure 1.1 The social structure of Anglo-Saxon England.

- Slaves
- Peasant farmers
- Thegns

1.1 Anglo-Saxon society

Extend your knowledge

Thegns

Thegns were divided into king's thegns, who held their land direct from the king and served him directly, and those who held their land from earls and other thegns.

When a man became a thegn, he paid a tax called a heriot. Heriot meant 'war gear' and the tax required a thegn to equip himself with a helmet and coat of mail, a horse and harness, and a sword and spear.

Earls

Earls* were the most important aristocrats: the most important men in the country after the king. The relationship between the king and his earls was based on loyalty. The earls competed against each other to be the one the king trusted and relied on the most, so that the king would give them the greatest rewards and honour. Sometimes, earls even challenged the king to get more power.

Key term

Earls*

Highest Anglo-Saxon aristocracy. The word came from the Danish 'jarl' and meant a chieftain who ruled a region on behalf of the king. The area controlled by an earl is called an earldom.

Changing social status

In other parts of Europe, such as in Normandy, people's status in society depended on ancestry: the importance of their family and ancestors. Anglo-Saxon society was much less rigid than this.

- A peasant who prospered and obtained five hides of land that he paid tax on could gain the status of a thegn.
- Merchants who made a number of trips abroad in their own ships could also become thegns.
- Slaves could be freed by their masters – and free peasants could sell themselves into slavery as a desperate measure to feed their families.
- At the top of the social system, thegns could be raised to the status of earls (and earls could be demoted to thegns). Earls could sometimes even become kings.

Exam-style question, Section B

Describe **two** features of the social system of Anglo-Saxon England. **4 marks**

Exam tip

This question is about identifying key features. You need to identify two relevant points and then develop each point. For example: 'The social system was not fixed. This meant a free peasant who did very well could become a thegn.'

Extend your knowledge

Anglo-Saxon England

The areas of Britain controlled by Anglo-Saxons had changed over the centuries. Viking invasions had taken control of vast areas, which had then been recaptured. Anglo-Saxon England also had hostile neighbours: Wales, Scotland and Ireland and, to the south, Normandy. The location of Normandy is included on this map, but it was never under Anglo-Saxon control.

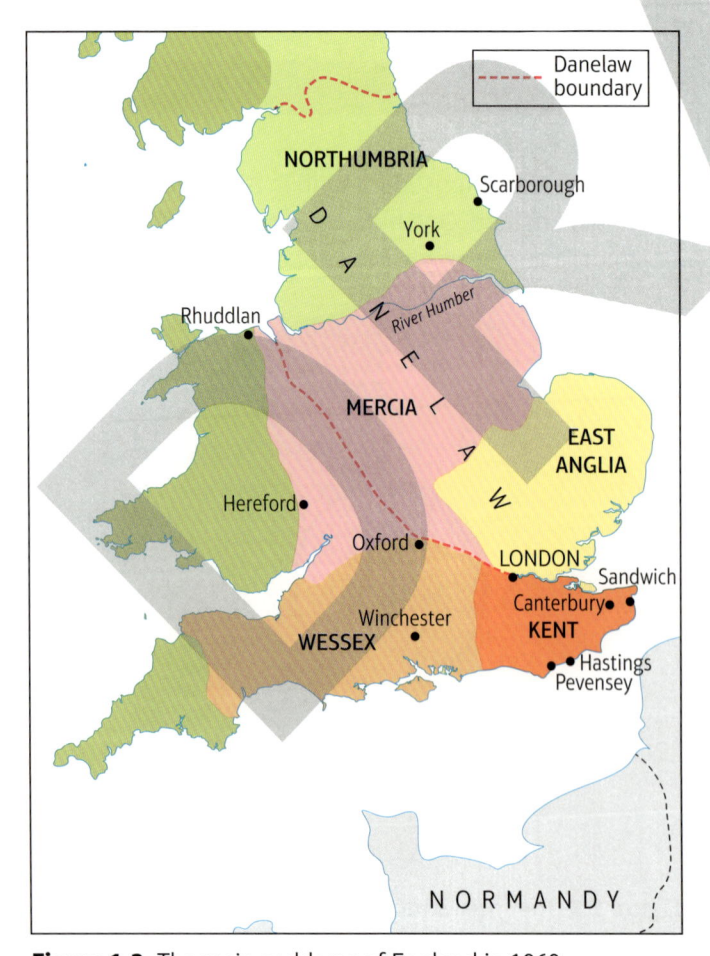

Figure 1.2 The main earldoms of England in 1060.

The power of the English monarchy

In 1060, the king (monarch) was Edward the Confessor. He was the most powerful person in Anglo-Saxon England. He governed the country.

Powers of the king

- **Law-making**: the king created new laws and made sure they were enforced throughout the country.
- **Money**: the king controlled the production of the silver pennies used as money.
- **Landownership**: the king owned large estates and could grant land out to his followers. He could also take land away from those who had acted against him.
- **Military power**: the king had the ability to raise a national army and fleet.
- **Taxation**: the king decided when taxes should be paid and a national taxation system delivered this tax to him.

Duties of the people

- To obey the law as it was passed down through the king's local representatives.
- To use the king's coins. Forging coins was a very serious crime.
- Land carried with it obligations to the king. The main two obligations were payment of tax and military service.
- Landholders had to provide and equip fighters for the army or fleet; otherwise they were fined or lost their land.
- Landholders had to pay their taxes, otherwise they were fined or lost their land.

Figure 1.3 The powers of Edward the Confessor and the duties of his people. The image in the middle is a representation of Edward's royal seal. This was attached to his royal orders to show they came from the king.

The king's role was to protect his people from attack and give them laws to maintain safety and security at home. In return, the people of England owed him service. Every boy swore an oath* when they reached 12 years of age to be faithful to the king. The oath was administered by the shire reeve* at a special ceremony held each year (see Source A).

Source A

The oath sworn by Anglo-Saxon boys once they reached 12 years of age.

All shall swear in the name of the Lord, before whom every holy thing is holy, that they will be faithful to the king... From the day on which this oath shall be rendered, no one shall conceal the breach of it on the part of a brother or family relation, any more than in a stranger.

How powerful was Edward the Confessor?

Kings of Anglo-Saxon England held their power ultimately because they led armies. Anglo-Saxon kings had clawed England back from Viking control. Edward the Confessor was not a warrior king, but his earls and their thegns were a powerful military force and he relied on his earls, especially Earl Godwin, to protect England from attack.

Kings who were war leaders gained legitimacy for their rule because they could hand out the wealth and land of their defeated enemies to their followers. When kings did not have success in battle then their power could be reduced. However, Edward had other reasons that made him a legitimate king.

Key terms

Oath*

A solemn promise to do something. Anglo-Saxons swore oaths on holy relics to make them especially binding. A relic was often a body part of a dead saint, kept in a special casket.

Shire reeve*

An official of the king: his sheriff. Sheriffs managed the king's estates, collected revenue for him and were in charge of local courts.

1.1 Anglo-Saxon society

- **He was a respected law-maker.** Anglo-Saxon society as a whole valued kings who kept things peaceful, because quarrels between families were common and could frequently break out into fighting that threatened everyone in a community.
- **He was pious (very religious).** Anglo-Saxon kings claimed a special link to God: they were anointed* as a representative of Christ on Earth. It was believed that a worthy king could bring God's blessing to his country and that God could also guide his actions.

Key term

Anointed*

To put sacred oil on someone as part of a religious ceremony.

Limits to the king's power

Anglo-Saxon kings needed to rule the whole of England, but half the country, called the Danelaw*, was Anglo-Danish. Many of its inhabitants were the descendants of Viking invaders. Although they accepted Edward's rule, people wanted to be ruled by local men and to follow their own laws and customs.

While the Danelaw area represented an administrative challenge, Edward the Confessor's real problems were with Earl Godwin of Wessex. Wessex was the richest earldom of England and Godwin and his family owned so much land that they were as rich as the king. They were lords to so many thegns that they were militarily much more powerful than the king. While Anglo-Saxon society viewed disloyalty to your lord as the ultimate crime, there was no reason why Godwin should not try to put pressure on the king to do things his way. For example, to appoint some of Godwin's men to important Church positions or give earldoms to his sons.

Tensions between Godwin and Edward had come to a head in 1050. The king had ordered Godwin to punish the people of Dover after a visiting embassy from Boulogne was attacked. Godwin had refused. As a result, Edward, with the help of two other important earls, Siward of Northumbria and Leofric of Mercia, forced Godwin into exile. But, in 1051, Godwin returned with a fleet and an army. He asked Edward if his earldom could be restored to him. To prevent war, Edward agreed.

Activities

1. While you are at school, your teacher (your lord) provides you with education and looks after your well-being. What duties do you owe your teacher in return?
2. Describe two features of Anglo-Saxon monarchy that enabled the king to protect England from foreign invasions.
3. Explain two ways in which 'over-mighty' earls, like Earl Godwin, could challenge the king's power. Use the example of Godwin's refusal to punish those responsible for the fight in Dover to help you make a convincing argument.

Key term

The Danelaw*

The part of England where Danish (Viking) power had been strongest and which had kept some of its Danish laws instead of Anglo-Saxon ones. You can see the area occupied by the Danelaw in Figure 1.2.

Government

The Witan

The Witan was a council that advised the king on issues of government. It was made up of the most important aristocrats of the kingdom, including earls and archbishops. It discussed:

- possible threats from foreign powers
- religious affairs
- land disputes and how to settle them.

The Witan also had an important role in approving a new king, which will be looked at later (page 27).

The king did not have to follow the Witan's advice. The king also decided who was appointed to the Witan and when it was to meet.

1.1 Anglo-Saxon society

Source A

The king and his Witan. This image is from an 11th-century book of Old Testament Bible stories. It is useful for historians of Anglo-Saxon England because the artists have portrayed the Old Testament king as though he was an Anglo-Saxon king, surrounded by his advisors.

Earldoms

What power did earls have?

Earldoms had been introduced by the Viking king of England, Cnut, after he had invaded and conquered Anglo-Saxon England in 1015. At first, Cnut made his followers the earls of four great earldoms, but he soon passed the title on to the leader of the most important family in each earldom. For example, Cnut made Godwin Earl of Wessex in the 1030s. Godwin was not a Dane, like Cnut – he was an Anglo-Saxon thegn from Sussex. However, Godwin had shown he was a man that Cnut could trust to follow him loyally.

In order to aid the king in governing the country, the earls were given many of the powers of the king.

- They were responsible for collecting the taxes of their earldom and they received a share of all the revenue collected. This share was very large – a third – and it meant that earls were rich. They were supposed to use this economic power to ensure their earldom was well defended and well run.

- They oversaw justice and legal punishments in their earldom. Most types of crime came under their jurisdiction (the things they were responsible for): there were only a few crimes that only the king could judge. This gave the earls strong social powers: controlling and influencing the way people lived.

- They had great military power. They were the lords to many hundreds of thegns, and also maintained an elite bodyguard of professional soldiers called housecarls*. The king therefore used his earls like generals: they were his military leaders against the king's enemies.

These powers gave the earls economic, legal and military control of their earldoms. The big earldoms (see Figure 1.2) formed enormous 'power bases' for their earls.

Key term

Housecarls*

Highly-trained troops that stayed with their lord wherever he went; a bodyguard.

15

1.1 Anglo-Saxon society

Limits to the earls' powers

When a king was strong, as Cnut was for most of his reign, the power of the earls was definitely less than that of the king. A powerful king like Cnut would demand obedience and would punish those who failed him. But a king like Edward the Confessor was not so strong. He had spent most of his life in exile and did not have the backing of hundreds of important followers in England. It seems likely that he had to depend on Earl Godwin in particular. When Edward brought Normans into important positions in English government, Godwin and the other earls resisted their appointments and worked to get the Normans sent home again.

However, the earls' power relied on the support of the thegns in their earldoms. We know this because of occasions when thegns demanded that earls be removed from their positions. This happened in 1065 when Earl Tostig, the son of Godwin, lost his earldom and went into exile after protests from his thegns about the way he governed his earldom, Northumbria.

> ### Extend your knowledge
>
> **Earl Tostig**
>
> Tostig Godwinson was made Earl of Northumbria, a huge earldom, in 1055. Tostig was earl for ten years and he took his responsibility to keep law and order very seriously. Northumbria was plagued by bandits, who laid in wait for travellers and robbed them, often killing their victims. Tostig ordered that all such men be hunted down and either killed (if they were ordinary people) or mutilated (if they were from important families). This decisive action meant that people were soon able to travel safely again, until Tostig was exiled in 1065 and law and order broke down once more.
>
> However, Tostig did not only use his powers to make his earldom safer for travellers. He also used them to benefit himself. He did this by warning rich families that they would be accused of being bandits unless they paid him money.
>
> Tostig's example shows that the powers of the earl could be very useful for saving major problems in an earldom, but they could also prove a threat to good government if they were misused.

Local government

The shire, the hundred and the hide

Earldoms were divided into shires. Shires had social, political, economic and military functions.

- **Social:** each shire had its own court for trying cases and giving punishments.
- **Political:** the shire reeve acted as the king's representative in the shire (see below).
- **Economic:** each shire had a burh (fortified town) as its main administrative and trading centre.
- **Military:** each shire provided troops for the fyrd* (see below).

Shires were divided into **hundreds***, and hundreds into **tithings*** – units of ten households. At the base of the whole administrative system was the hide. Each hide of land carried obligations: payment of taxes and military service.

> ### Key terms
>
> **Fyrd***
>
> The men of the Anglo-Saxon army and fleet. Every five hides provided one man for the fyrd.
>
> **Hundreds***
>
> A unit of land administration. In some parts of England, a hundred was 100 hides of land, but in other areas it didn't have this direct connection.
>
> **Tithings***
>
> An administrative unit that was a group of ten households – originally equivalent to a tenth of a hundred in some areas.

> ### Exam-style question, Section B
>
> Describe **two** features of earldoms in Anglo-Saxon England. **4 marks**

> ### Exam tip
>
> A feature is something that is distinctive or characteristic – we distinguish one person from another, for example, by recognising their distinctive facial features. So, when a question asks for two features of earldoms, think about the things that made earldoms distinctive – their special characteristics. Remember to develop each point to explain the feature.

1.1 Anglo-Saxon society

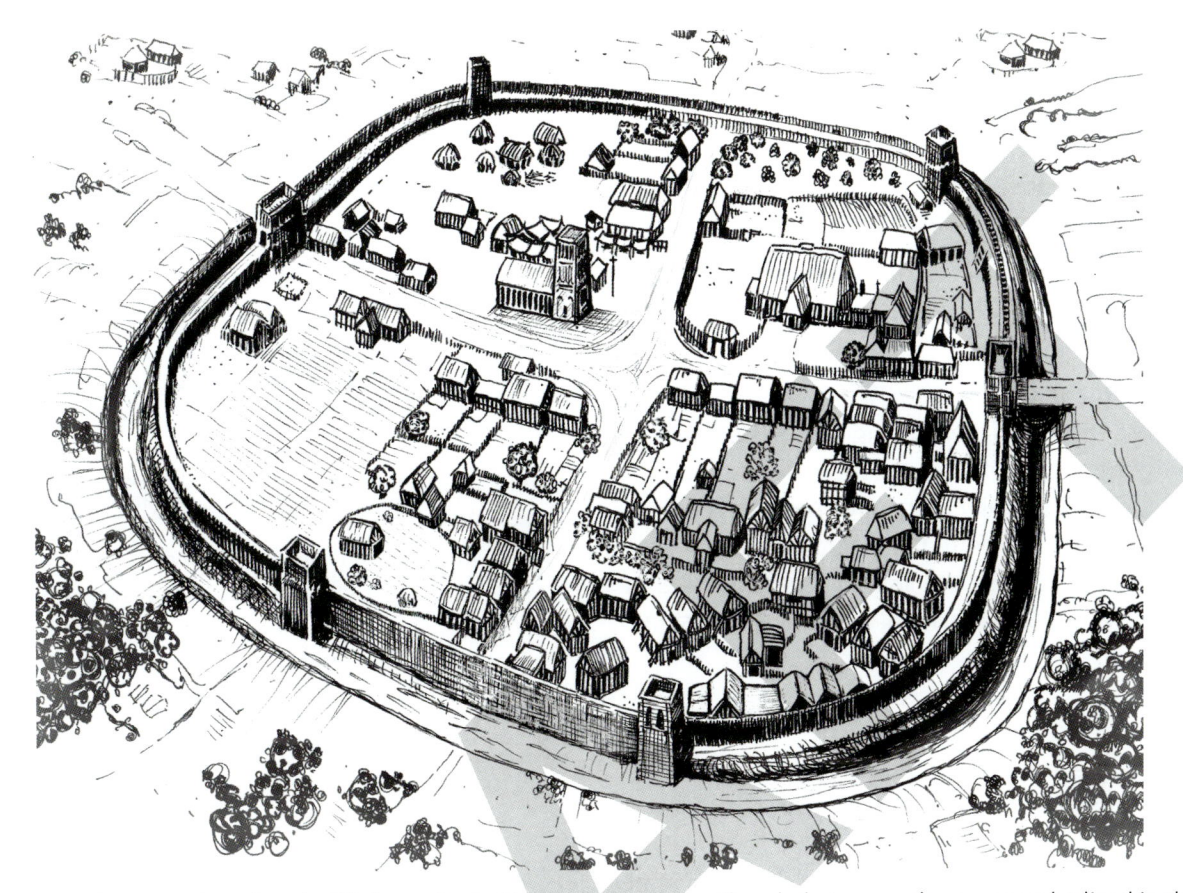

Figure 1.4 Artist's impression of an Anglo-Saxon burh. Strong walls enclose the whole town and everyone who lived in the burh shared responsibilities for maintaining the defences.

Shire reeves

The shire reeves, or sheriffs, were the king's local government officials and they worked within the earldoms to look after the king's interests and carry out his instructions. Their duties included:

- collecting revenues from the king's land
- collecting the geld tax*
- collecting fines from the shire court
- enforcing and witnessing the law at the shire court
- responsibilities for providing men for the fyrd and for the upkeep of roads and fortifications.

The king issued his orders to the shire reeves through writs. These were written instructions with a seal stamped by the king.

Key term

Geld tax*

A tax on land, originally to pay off the Vikings (Danegeld). It went to the king.

Military service – the fyrd

When the call came from the king, each group of five hides was obliged to provide one man for the fyrd, together with his battle equipment. Some historians argue that there were two types of fyrd:

- The **select** fyrd gathered men to fight anywhere in England for the king.
- The **general** fyrd gathered men to fight who didn't travel outside their local area.

The select fyrd was made up of thegns and their followers, rather than the general populace. The thegns probably trained together and were well-equipped with weapons, armour and horses. However, these men could only stay away from home for so long before the management of their farms would suffer – especially at harvest time, when lots of people were needed to cut the crops and bring them into storage. A period of 40 days was therefore fixed for their service, after which a fyrd would be disbanded.

1.1 Anglo-Saxon society

> **Extend your knowledge**
>
> **The fyrd**
> By 1060, the system had evolved so that, instead of providing the troops themselves, the hundreds could pay a fee instead. That money was then used to hire professional soldiers.

The legal system

The king and the law
The king was the law-maker, issuing laws to fulfil his role of keeping the peace. Offences against the king's peace, such as robbing a traveller, were punished harshly. The people of England looked to the king to provide peace. The people also expected the king to provide justice: to treat everyone of the same social standing in the same way.

Blood feuds and Wergild
Traditionally, if a family member was attacked, then the rest of the family would find the person responsible and punish them. This led to blood feuds*. Feuds could continue for generations and they could spread to affect whole communities.

The solution to the blood feud problem was Wergild. Instead of taking revenge, the family who had suffered the murder were paid compensation by the murderer's family. The Wergild system showed a commitment to fairness in Anglo-Saxon society as it gave equal status to all people of a certain social standing. However, it also shows the importance of status.

- A ceorl was worth 20 shillings.
- A thegn was worth 1,200 shillings.
- An earl or an archbishop was worth 3,600 shillings.

It is difficult to make direct comparisons with our money today, but some historians suggest 1 shilling was equivalent to £100 today.

> **Key term**
>
> **Blood feuds***
> A revenge system based on family loyalties and honour. If someone was killed, the victim's family had the right to kill someone from the murderer's family, who then had the right to revenge themselves, and so on.

Collective responsibility
When a crime was committed, it was the duty of all members of a tithing to hunt for the criminal: this was called the 'hue and cry'. The men of the tithing were also responsible for the good behaviour of their ten households. If someone was proved to have done something wrong, they had to pay a fine. If, for example, someone from their village refused to join the general fyrd, there would be consequences for everyone in the tithing. This community-based justice system followed a principle called 'collective responsibility'.

> **Activities**
>
> 1. Imagine that your class is divided into groups of ten and that you are collectively responsible for each other's behaviour. What are the advantages of this system for your teacher and the school? Are there any disadvantages to the system?
> 2. Come up with one strength and one weakness of the fyrd system for defending Anglo-Saxon England from attack.
> 3. Describe how each of the following was involved in the government of Anglo-Saxon England. Which one was most important, in your view? Explain your answer.
>   a. Earls
>   b. Shire reeves
>   c. Geld tax
>   d. The Witan

The Anglo-Saxon economy

Historians are not entirely sure about what England produced that enabled it to trade so effectively; wool and cloth products are likely to have been the most important products because we know they were vital to English trade later in the medieval period. Western England was particularly well-suited to sheep rearing. Eastern England had drier conditions and fertile soils that made it excellent for arable farming (growing crops). Farming was well-organised: for example, there were over 6,000 mills throughout the country used for grinding the local community's grain into flour.

Most of the silver used to make Anglo-Saxon coins came from Germany, rather than being mined in Britain. Silver was very valuable, so England must have been able to export products that had high value abroad to be able to import silver from Germany.

1.1 Anglo-Saxon society

There is also evidence of other products from Europe being used in Anglo-Saxon England, including millstones (used in Anglo-Saxon mills) and whetstones (used to sharpen blades) from Denmark, and wine from Normandy.

Source C

An Anglo-Saxon silver penny from Edward the Confessor's reign. The coin shows Edward sitting on his throne. He is holding an orb (the ball-shaped object) and a sceptre: symbols of royalty that are still used by British monarchy today.

Extend your knowledge

Making coins
The king controlled the process of minting (making) coins. Coins had to be a standard thickness and weight. The metal stamps that were used to make the coins were issued from a central location controlled by the king. There were harsh punishments for any forging.

Towns

By the end of Edward's reign in 1066, something like 10% of the population of England lived in towns. Each shire had its main town. These fortified burhs had been planned so that no one was more than 15 or 20 miles from safety if news of a Viking raiding party reached them. They were linked by roads so that troops could move quickly from one burh to another.

They had strong walls and ramparts (steep earth banks) guarded by men from the town (see Figure 1.4). Administration and upkeep of the town and its fortifications was the responsibility of the burh's inhabitants.

Towns and trade

The burhs were also trading hubs. The king's laws demanded that all trade worth more than a set amount of money should take place in a burh, so that trade tax could be paid. By 1060, London and York were the biggest cities in England, with populations of more than 10,000 people. Towns like Norwich and Lincoln had populations of around 6,000.

Towns often grew in importance because of international trading links. York was a centre for trade with Denmark, for example; Bristol was the centre of trade between the west of England and Viking settlements in southern Ireland. London was probably the biggest trading hub of all, with documents from the time listing the presence in London of traders from Germany, France, Normandy and Flanders. These traders would have taken back reports about England to their own countries.

Villages

Historians think that many of the villages in England today began in Anglo-Saxon times, but not as a cluster of houses grouped around a church, surrounded by the village's fields. Villages were more likely to be a large number of quite isolated homes and farms scattered over the countryside. The houses were made of wood and thatched with straw, and were homes for lots of relatives living together rather than just one family. Most thegns lived in the countryside too. Their manor houses were larger and better built than peasant huts. Some of these manor houses may have been fortified against attack. Thegns often built a church on their land, too, and employed a priest to hold services for the thegn's household. These churches would also provide services for the surrounding area. It was connections to the local thegn and to the local church that brought people together into a village.

The influence of the Church

There were many reforms to Church teachings and practice happening in Europe by 1060 but, unlike in Normandy, English bishops were not very involved in these changes. The English Church was traditional-minded, resistant to reform, and it focused on Anglo-Saxon saints as well as older Celtic saints. These Anglo-Saxon and Celtic saints were often linked to a local area and were saints that the local people felt were familiar: part of their everyday lives.

1.1 Anglo-Saxon society

The Church was organised into large areas, each controlled by a bishop. The bishops were often rich, important people. Bishops served on the Witan as the king's advisers. Norman sources paint some English bishops as being corrupt: selling Church jobs for profit, though this may have been unfair in some cases. There was a tension between bishops and the churches set up by thegns: bishops did not want local priests being hired and fired by anyone else except them. Gradually, these local priests and their parishes were brought under the bishops' control.

Local priests were usually quite ordinary members of the community. They were not especially well-educated (many could not read Latin, the language of the Church), they had small landholdings like peasants and they were usually married, which went against the reforms that required priests to be celibate (single, and not involved in sexual relationships).

England also had monasteries and nunneries: religious communities of monks and nuns headed by abbots and abbesses. Unlike in Normandy, monasteries were in decline. Numbers were shrinking and, in the monasteries that survived, monks formed part of their local communities rather than living separate, holy lives apart from the world.

Religion in Anglo-Saxon England was an important part of everyday life. The influence of the Church was very strong because people were worried about what would happen when they died. Everyone believed that they would spend time in the afterlife being punished for their sins, and participating in religious activity and prayer provided a way for people to reduce this period of punishment.

Religion was important to King Edward, who devoted much of his later years to rebuilding Westminster cathedral, and also to people's idea of what a king was for. The king was an agent of God, and his conduct and rule had to reflect this. Contemporary sources show that English people believed God would be quick to punish countries for the sinful behaviour of their people, especially sinfulness within the Church or monarchy.

Activity

Focused listing is a useful study skill to develop. Here's how it works:
a Write out the main Topic headings, e.g. Anglo-Saxon society, The power of the monarchy, Government, etc.
b For each one, read quickly through the text and then close the book.
c Then, for each heading, make a list of the main terms and ideas you can recall about it.
d Check back through the book to see what you left out.
Use this method to make notes on the 'Government' and 'Economy' sections.

Summary

- Although most Anglo-Saxons were 'free' (except slaves), everyone had obligations and duties to someone higher up.
- The king was very powerful and made the laws governing England.
- Local government and local justice was administered by local people and officials.
- England had a strong economy and an effective tax system.

Checkpoint

Strengthen

S1 Describe the differences between slaves, ceorls (free famers), thegns and earls.
S2 Write a paragraph on 'a day in the life of a shire reeve'. Think about the duties that they were expected to perform.
S3 Explain what each of the following was: geld tax, the fyrd, a burh.

Challenge

C1 Summarise three ways in which the Anglo-Saxon king was more powerful than his earls.
C2 Explain why thegns were important in Anglo-Saxon England.
How confident do you feel about your answers to these questions? If you are not sure that you have answered them well, try the above study skills activity.

1.2 The last years of Edward the Confessor and the succession crisis

Learning outcomes

- Understand the power and position of the House of Godwin.
- Understand the significance of Harold's embassy to Normandy.
- Understand the reasons for and results of the rising against Tostig.

Timeline
The last years of Edward the Confessor

- **1053** Death of Earl Godwin; Harold Godwinson becomes Earl of Wessex
- **1055** Tostig Godwinson made Earl of Northumbria
- **1062** The Godwins defeat the Welsh king, Gruffudd ap Llywelyn
- **1064** Harold's embassy to Normandy
- **1065** Uprising against Earl Tostig; Tostig exiled
- **1066** Death of Edward the Confessor; Harold becomes king

The house of Godwin

The house of Godwin* began in 1018 during King Cnut's reign, when Cnut made his favourite advisor, Godwin, Earl of Wessex. Godwin was probably the son of an Anglo-Saxon thegn.

Key term

House of Godwin*

The 'house' of Godwin refers to the Godwin family. The current British royal family is the house of Windsor, for example.

Extend your knowledge

King Cnut

Cnut was king of England from 1016 to 1035. When he took control of England, he executed leading Anglo-Saxons who might have led rebellions against his rule. Then he began to promote Anglo-Saxons he could trust alongside his Danish followers.

Political power in Anglo-Saxon England had strong family connections. Godwin had helped Edward the Confessor to become king and, in return, the king married Godwin's daughter, Edith of Wessex, in 1045. That family link to the throne was very significant in Anglo-Saxon society. Brothers-in-laws of kings had succeeded to the throne in the past.

Harold's succession as Earl of Wessex

When Godwin died in 1053, his family's influence was reduced as rival earls jostled for position. However, the Godwins built up their control again. By the mid-1060s the Godwins had control of almost all England.

- Harold Godwinson succeeded his father as Earl of Wessex, giving him riches, influence over hundreds of thegns and a powerful position as adviser to the king.
- In 1055, Tostig Godwinson (Harold's brother) became the new Earl of Northumbria. That gave the Godwins a powerbase in the far north of England.
- In 1057, the earldom of East Anglia was given to Gyrth Godwinson, Harold's teenage brother.
- Also in 1057, a smaller earldom in the southwest Midlands went to Leofwine Godwinson – another younger brother of Harold.

Why did Edward the Confessor allow the Godwins to increase their power so extensively?

- Edward's marriage to Edith was certainly important, making him kin to the Godwins.
- England was under threat from Norway, meaning that Edward needed his earls to be strong military leaders. That is probably the reason why Tostig was made Earl of Northumbria instead of the old earl's son, Waltheof, who was too young to lead men into battle.
- Harold's marriage to Edith the Fair (another Edith) may also have influenced the Godwins' gaining East Anglia, as she is thought to have inherited large estates in that region.

21

1.2 The last years of Edward the Confessor and the succession crisis

Military success

The only significant rival to the Godwins left in England by the 1060s was Aelfgar, Earl of Mercia. He was exiled twice in the 1050s, teaming up with the Welsh king, Gruffudd ap Llywelyn, both times to fight for the return of his earldom. When Aelfgar died, probably in 1062, King Edward and the Godwins acted swiftly. They didn't want Llywelyn working with rivals again to challenge their interests. After a surprise attack in 1062, which Llywelyn escaped, Harold took a fleet round the coast of South Wales while Tostig led an army overland into North Wales.

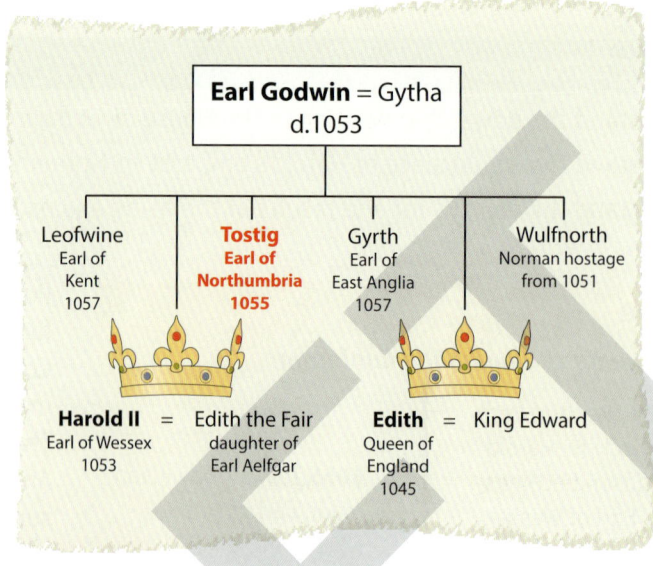

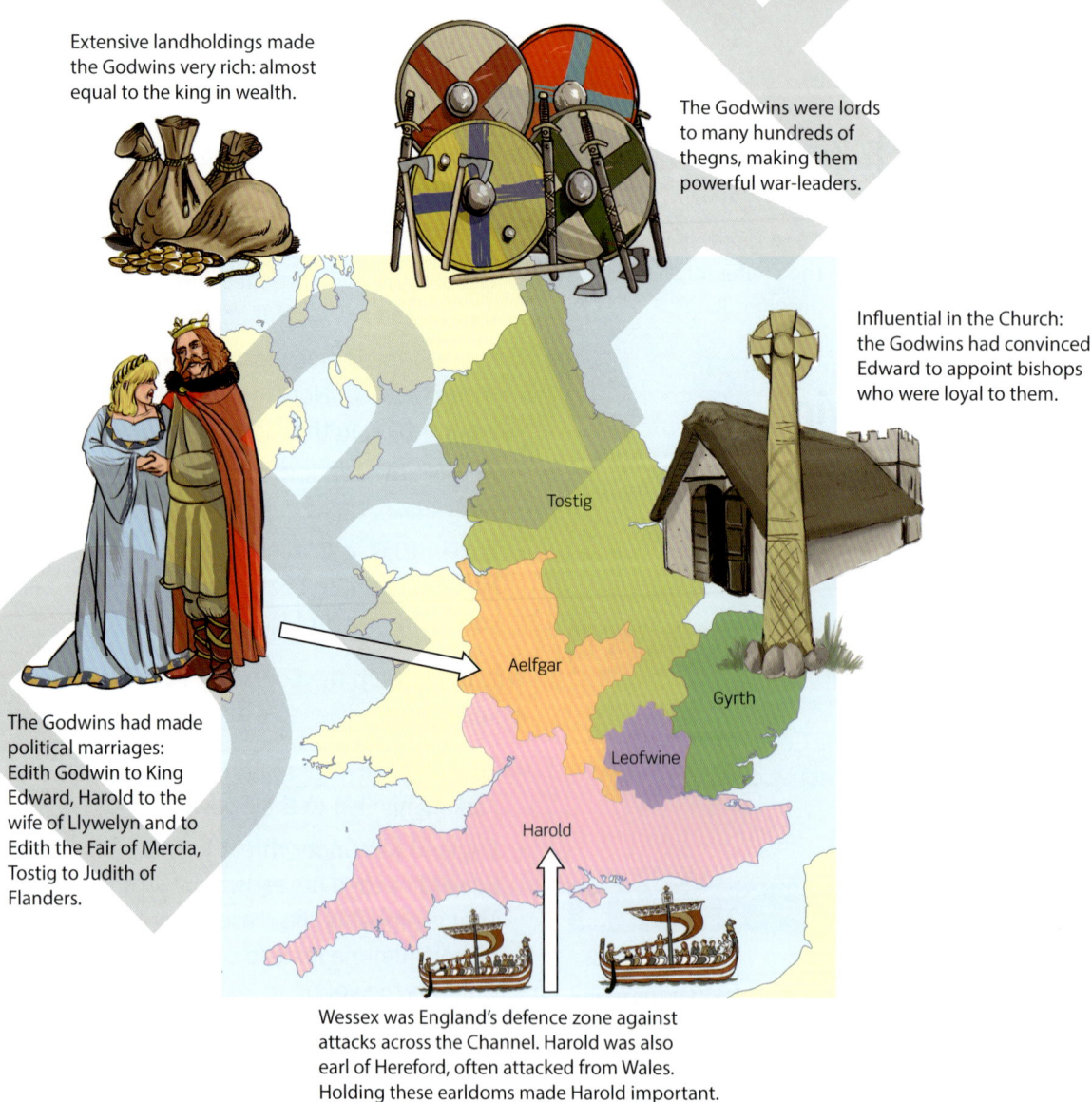

Earl Godwin = Gytha
d.1053

- Leofwine, Earl of Kent 1057
- **Tostig, Earl of Northumbria 1055**
- Gyrth, Earl of East Anglia 1057
- Wulfnorth, Norman hostage from 1051

Harold II = Edith the Fair, Earl of Wessex 1053, daughter of Earl Aelfgar

Edith = King Edward, Queen of England 1045

Extensive landholdings made the Godwins very rich: almost equal to the king in wealth.

The Godwins were lords to many hundreds of thegns, making them powerful war-leaders.

Influential in the Church: the Godwins had convinced Edward to appoint bishops who were loyal to them.

The Godwins had made political marriages: Edith Godwin to King Edward, Harold to the wife of Llywelyn and to Edith the Fair of Mercia, Tostig to Judith of Flanders.

Wessex was England's defence zone against attacks across the Channel. Harold was also earl of Hereford, often attacked from Wales. Holding these earldoms made Harold important.

Figure 1.5 The power of the Godwins in 1060.

1.2 The last years of Edward the Confessor and the succession crisis

Their joint strategy was a brilliant success. Harold sent Llywelyn's head to Edward the Confessor, but it was Harold himself who appointed a new 'puppet' king for Wales whom he could control. Harold had assumed the role of '*sub regulus*' – the king's deputy, leader of his armies: by far the most powerful of Edward's earls.

Godwin and the king

Edward showed signs earlier in his reign of trying to shake off Godwin's control. In 1042, he had appointed some Normans to influential positions, causing conflict with aristocrats like Godwin. Norman sources insist that Edward promised the English throne to William of Normandy after his death, in return for William's support against Godwin. What's not clear, however, is what help, if any, was given from Normandy: Godwin was returned to power in 1051 without any intervention from Normandy, and his sons were given the most powerful positions in the kingdom.

Extend your knowledge

Edward and Normandy

What we know of as France today was not the same in 1060. Normandy, part of France today, was then an independent dukedom. The duke of Normandy owed duty to the king of France, but that did not stop regular wars between them, or between Normandy and other counties such as Flanders, Boulogne and Brittany. In fact, Normandy had once been part of Brittany.

Edward the Confessor had a close relationship with Normandy. Edward's mother, Emma, was from Normandy and, when Vikings seized the throne of England, Edward went into exile there in 1016. He lived there for 25 years.

When Edward became king of England in 1043, he brought with him favourites of his from Normandy. Anglo-Saxon England and Normandy were very well connected by 1060.

Activities

1. Identify one way in which the Godwins were economically powerful, one way in which they were militarily powerful and one way in which they were politically powerful.
2. Give three pieces of evidence or extra information to explain each of the three choices you made in question 1.
3. Edward the Confessor was 57 in 1060: an old man in Anglo-Saxon times. To what extent do you think the Godwins became so powerful because Edward was not strong enough to control them? Or do you think the Godwins helped Edward to rule England successfully? Write up your answer after discussing it with a partner. Make sure you back up your points with evidence and reach a decision on these questions at the end of your answer.

Harold's embassy to Normandy

Harold Godwinson went to Normandy in the early summer of 1064 (or possibly 1065) on a mission for King Edward – a type of visit called an embassy.

Harold travelled to France, but landed in Ponthieu, a small county between Normandy and Flanders – perhaps blown off-course by a storm. Harold was taken prisoner by Count Guy of Ponthieu, but Duke William heard of the capture and demanded that Guy hand Harold over. Harold then spent time with William in Normandy, and helped him in two military campaigns, which resulted in William giving Harold gifts of weapons and armour. These gifts were symbolic of the relationship between a lord and his warrior.

After relaying King Edward's message to William (it's unknown what that message was), Harold made a solemn oath to William, swearing on two holy relics. This could have been an oath of allegiance: Harold swearing to support William's claim to the throne of England.

1.2 The last years of Edward the Confessor and the succession crisis

Anglo-Saxon and Norman interpretations of why he went on this mission differ.

- The Norman interpretation of the visit was that King Edward commissioned Harold to go to talk to Duke William about plans for William's succession, and that the visit involved Harold swearing allegiance to him as his future king.
- The Anglo-Saxon interpretation is that Harold went to recover two hostages* from William – Harold's brother and his nephew, Wulfnorth and Hakon.

> **Key term**
>
> **Hostages***
>
> People given to another as part of an oath or agreement. If the oath or agreement was broken, the hostages could be killed or maimed [e.g. have hands cut off, be blinded (or both)].

Harold's embassy to Normandy is difficult to interpret, but it is significant in three main ways:

- It shows that Harold was King Edward's trusted advisor, as this was clearly an important embassy, whatever its overall aim actually was.
- It was used by the Normans to boost William's claim to the throne. Even if the embassy was not about William becoming king of England, it suggests close ties between England and Normandy.
- It was used by the Normans to portray Harold as an oath-breaker after Harold became king instead of helping William to the throne of England. Even if Harold never actually swore allegiance to William, it is a useful indication of how important such oaths of allegiance between a lord and a follower were in both Anglo-Saxon and Norman society.

Source A

A scene from the Bayeux Tapestry, probably produced in Kent around 1070 on the orders of Bishop Odo of Bayeux. This scene shows Harold swearing an oath in William's presence.

1.2 The last years of Edward the Confessor and the succession crisis

The rising against Earl Tostig

Reasons for the rising

Tostig Godwinson became Earl of Northumbria in 1055 after the death of Earl Siward. Northumbria was an important earldom because it was very large (see Figure 1.5), it guarded the border with Scotland and had a long history of Viking attacks and settlement. Because it had a long association with the Vikings, and was a long way away from the powerbase of the Anglo-Saxon king in the south, it was the obvious place for Vikings to make new invasion attempts from.

Northumbria was very different from Wessex, the Godwin's powerbase in the south of England. Much of it was part of the Danelaw, the area that had been settled by the Vikings. There were some different laws and customs, hence 'Dane-law'. People in the Danelaw used lots of words borrowed from the Scandinavian languages of the Vikings. It is probable that a southerner, like Tostig, would have found understanding the Northumbrians difficult.

Earl Tostig ruled Northumbria for ten years. In October 1065, there was an uprising against Tostig, led by important Northumbrian thegns. There were several reasons for the rising:

Extend your knowledge

Danelaw differences

Danelaw differences were often more about similar things being called something different, for example the hundred was called the *wapentake* and a hide was called a *carucate* in the Danelaw.

Other differences were more significant. There were many more ceorls in the Danelaw part of England: peasants who were not bound in service to their lord and who could, if they wanted to, go and work for someone else. Also, because the geld tax had originally been used to pay Vikings not to attack England, the northern Danegeld regions paid taxes at a much lower rate than other parts of the country.

Map annotations:

- His personal friendship with Malcolm III, King of Scotland, meant he didn't defend Northumbria from Scottish attacks. While Tostig was away on pilgrimage in 1061, King Malcolm invaded Northumbria and caused much destruction. However, when Tostig returned, he did not launch an attack on Malcolm but, instead, agreed peace terms with him.
- He had been unjust - imposing new laws (from the south) and using his legal powers to get rid of rivals. Tostig's enemies complained that he abused his position to falsely accuse people of crimes in order to take money and land from them.
- He had taxed Northumbria too heavily - possibly to pay for the Godwins' war in Wales. Danelaw areas were not used to heavy taxation, so the Northumbrians resented this greatly.
- He had ordered the assassination of high-born Northumbrian rivals while they were his guests.
- Tostig was a southerner and Northumbria had always been governed by northerners; the southern kings of Anglo-Saxon England had generally left the north to govern itself with minimum interference.

Extend your knowledge

Northumbrian resentment

The resentment against Tostig had been building over many years, with most of the reasons for the rising being long-term ones: over-taxation and unfairness. The trigger for the rising in 1065 was Tostig's murder (in 1064) of two followers of Gospatric (a leading Northumbrian aristocrat) after Tostig had invited them to York. Soon after, Gospatric was himself assassinated after he had travelled south to King Edward's court to complain about Tostig to the king. This was viewed in Northumbria as the very worst kind of treachery.

The rising of 1065 began with rebels marching on York, the city from which Northumbria was governed. There, the rebels killed as many of Tostig's housecarls and servants as they could find, and declared Tostig an outlaw. They invited Morcar, the brother of the Earl of Mercia, to be their earl instead of Tostig.

1.2 The last years of Edward the Confessor and the succession crisis

Harold's response to the rising

King Edward held a conference to decide what to do about the rising. The outcome was surprising. Instead of raising an army to march north and defeat the rebels, Harold instead met with them and passed on King Edward's agreement to their terms. Harold married Morcar's sister (his second wife) and was given large landholdings in Mercia. The rising had begun at the start of October 1065. By 1 November, Tostig was exiled.

There are not enough sources to be sure exactly what happened, but the evidence seems to suggest that:

- Harold, like the king's other advisers, agreed that Tostig had pushed Northumbria too far: Tostig was to blame for the rising.
- Furious that Harold had not backed him, Tostig angrily accused Harold of having conspired against him, saying that the rising was a plot to replace him.
- King Edward commanded an army to be raised to put down the rising, but his command was not obeyed. Harold made excuses and the other earls did the same.
- Edward therefore had no choice but to accept the rebels' demands. Their choice of Morcar was diplomatic – another southerner, like Edward himself, when the rebels could have pushed for a Northumbrian, such as Waltheof, the son of their old earl, Siward.

Why would Harold have acted to weaken the house of Godwin and betray his brother? It is likely that Harold's ambitions were now greater than the interests of his family: he wanted to be king.

- Edward the Confessor was old and ill (he died three months after the Northumbrian rising).
- Harold needed a united kingdom to hold off the threats from Normandy and Scandinavia: a war with Mercia and Northumbria would weaken English defences.
- Tostig was a rival to the throne. Although his exile and enmity was probably something Harold regretted, it must have seemed a lesser evil than allowing him to challenge his ambition.

The powers of the king – revisited

It was very significant that the earls, led by Harold, failed to obey King Edward's command. Earls were bound by oaths of loyalty to their king and they were supposed to act as his military leaders.

The refusal to lead an army against the rebels therefore shows that the power of the king could sometimes be challenged: if the king was weak and if it was in the interests of all the major earls to act together.

Exam-style question, Section B

Explain why there was a rising against Earl Tostig in 1065.

You may use the following in your answer:
- the Danelaw
- taxation

You **must** also use information of your own. **12 marks**

Exam tip

'Explain why' questions require you to identify relevant points that you can link together to construct a convincing explanation. Take care not to simply tell the story of the rebellion, which would be description. Instead, link each point you make to the question through analysis.

Death of Edward the Confessor

Edward the Confessor had no children with his wife, Edith of Wessex, daughter of Earl Godwin. This meant that, when he died on 5 January 1066, there was a succession* crisis.

Key term

Succession* (to the throne)

The process that decides who should be the next king or queen and 'succeed' to the throne.

The Bayeux Tapestry shows the death of Edward at his palace in Westminster – a picture of this scene is on the next page. Edward is with a small circle of people: his wife Edith, who sits at his feet; Stigand, the Anglo-Saxon Archbishop of Canterbury; one of Edward's ministers and Harold. Other sources report that Edward is shown holding out his hand to Harold. Edward said to Harold: 'I commend this woman [Edith] with all the kingdom to your protection.' Harold understood this to mean that he was to be king - Harold II. However, there were others who thought they had better claims to the throne: a situation that made the year 1066 a very eventful one!

1.2 The last years of Edward the Confessor and the succession crisis

Source B

The death of Edward the Confessor, portrayed in the Bayeux Tapestry.

Activity ?

KWL is a strategy to help you take control of your own learning. It stands for Know – Want to know – Learned. This is how it works:

a Draw a table with three columns: 'Know', 'Want to know', 'Learned'.
b For any topic you are learning about, write down what you know about it already.
c Next, write down what else you'd like know, what questions you have about what you know.
d When you find out the answers, write them in the 'Learned' column.

Use this method to make notes on this section. Here's an example:

Know	Want to know	Learned
Tostig was from Wessex; Northumbria was different.	Why was Northumbria different?	Part of Northumbria in Danelaw. Different laws, different language, tax lower.

Summary

- The house of Godwin had become the real 'power behind the throne' in Anglo-Saxon England.
- Harold's embassy to Normandy and his decisions over Tostig had major consequences.
- Edward the Confessor died childless, causing a succession crisis.

Checkpoint

Strengthen

S1 When did: Harold become Earl of Wessex; Tostig get exiled; King Edward die?
S2 Describe two aspects of the house of Godwin that made them so powerful.

Challenge

C1 In your own words, summarise three reasons why you think Harold went against King Edward's wishes over the rising against Tostig.
C2 What else would it be useful to know about the consequences of Tostig's exile?

How confident do you feel about your answers to these questions? If you are not sure that you have answered them well, try the above study skills activity.

1.3 The rival claimants for the throne

> **Learning outcomes**
> - Understand the rival claims to the kingdom following Edward's death.
> - Understand the appointment and reign of Harold Godwinson.
> - Understand the reasons for and significance of the battles of Gate Fulford and Stamford Bridge.

Source A

Harold, as shown in the Bayeux tapestry.

Harold Godwinson (c1022–1066)

Harold Godwinson was on the spot when King Edward died, as were many of the leading men of the realm. He based his claim on the king's deathbed words, his family connection to him (brother-in-law), his role in recent years as the king's right-hand man, his influence with the earls and thegns, and his proven military prowess. But there were rival claimants to the succession.

Harold Godwinson	
Claim	Appointed as King Edward's successor by the king himself.
Strength of claim	Good – supported by witnesses, but ones loyal to Harold.
Chance of success	Excellent – Harold had the support required to be made king.

Edgar Aethling (c1051–c1126)

There was, in fact, already a natural-born heir to Edward the Confessor. This was Edgar the Aethling. As Edward's nephew, Edgar was directly descended from royal blood, shown by his title 'Aethling', which meant a prince of royal blood. Edward the Confessor and Harold Godwinsson had brought Edgar and his father back from Hungary in 1054, where they had gone as exiles after Cnut became king (for more on King Cnut see page 19). Edgar's father promptly died, leaving the six-year-old in Edward's care, although Edward did nothing we know of to boost Edgar's chance of succession. In 1066, the leading men of Anglo-Saxon England, the Witan, knew the threats from Scandinavia and Normandy were very serious and thought a teenage king was not the right choice in such troubled times.

Edgar Aethling	
Claim	Royal blood.
Strength of claim	Strong in theory, but he had no power to back it up.
Chance of success	Weak – although teenagers had become kings before, Anglo-Saxon England at this time needed a warrior-king to defend it against foreign threats.

1.3 The rival claimants for the throne

Harald Hardrada (c1015–1066)

Harald Hardrada was the king of Norway. He was a fearsome old Viking warrior, feared across Europe as well as in other Scandinavian countries. His nickname 'Hardrada' meant 'stern ruler'. His claim to the English throne was based on Viking secret deals and treaties. It is a complicated claim to understand: the key point is that Hardrada believed he had a good enough chance of succeeding to launch an invasion of England.

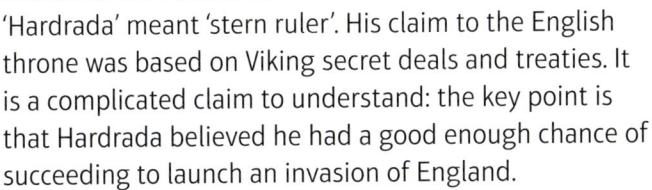

King Cnut (1016–1035) ruled England as part of a North Sea empire that included Denmark and Norway. When Cnut died, his son, Harthacnut, took the throne. However, shortly afterwards, Harthacnut lost control of Norway to Magnus Olafsson. To avoid war, they agreed a secret treaty that, in the event of one of them dying, the other would be their heir. When Harthacnut died in 1042, Magnus claimed the English throne as well as Harthacnut's Danish one.

Harald Hardrada's constant raiding parties along the Norwegian coast put so much pressure on Magnus that he offered to rule Norway together with Hardrada. This meant that, when Magnus died in 1047, Harald not only gained full control of Norway, he also took on Magnus' claim to England.

It is likely that Hardrada had no major plans to take up his complicated claim to the English throne when Edward the Confessor died. However, this changed when Tostig Godwinson, exiled from England, turned to Hardrada for support. Tostig gave Hardrada the impression that his brother, Harold, was very unpopular in England, especially in the north. Perhaps Tostig also convinced the old Viking that this was his chance for one last glorious adventure.

Harald Hardrada	
Claim	Based on a secret deal about another secret deal made by other Vikings!
Strength of claim	Weak, although the Danelaw might welcome a Viking king.
Chance of success	Good, as Harald had perhaps 15,000 warriors and 300 or more Viking longships at his command (together with Tostig's 12 ships), all very used to invading across the North Sea.

William of Normandy (c1028–1087)

William was Duke of Normandy, a small country (the size of Yorkshire) surrounded by enemies. He had fought hard to survive since he was very young. England offered the chance of real wealth and power to realise the Normans' ambitious plans throughout Europe.

His claim was based on an agreement William said was made between Edward the Confessor and himself around 1051, an agreement that was then supposedly confirmed by Harold's embassy to Normandy in 1064. William had come to England and Edward had promised him his throne, perhaps if Edward died childless. William managed to obtain the pope's backing for his claim, which proved very important in getting the support William needed for his invasion.

Extend your knowledge

Edward and William

Different historians have different interpretations of this agreement. Some deny that any such agreement was possible, others say that Edward was actually a Norman king anyway: he'd grown up in Normandy, modelled Westminster cathedral on Norman cathedrals, and tried to introduce Normans into positions of power when he began his reign in England. Edward certainly needed allies at the time, so it seems logical that he might have made some promises to William.

William of Normandy	
Claim	An agreement with King Edward.
Strength of claim	Backed by the pope, but lacking evidence.
Chance of success	Quite good: the Normans were Europe's best warriors, but William would have to find a way to convince his men to risk everything on a very risky invasion attempt and then get his men across the Channel.

29

1.3 The rival claimants for the throne

In Anglo-Saxon England, the king could not simply announce his successor: the Witan had a role in selecting the new king. It seems unlikely that the Witan would have accepted William in January 1066: Edward's attempt to bring Normans into senior positions earlier in his reign had been opposed very strongly by all the leading earls, many of whom were still in the Witan.

Activity

Divide the class into three groups: Group 1 are Anglo-Saxon actors performing 'The death of Edward the Confessor'; Group 2 is the court of Harald Hardrada; Group 3 is the court of William of Normandy.

a Group 1 needs to plan what their performance is going to show and what they're going to say, before performing it to Groups 2 and 3.

b Groups 2 and 3 need to explain their reactions to the performance to the other groups.

Harold's coronation and reign

Harold Godwinson's coronation (the ceremony where he was crowned king) took place the same day as Edward was buried: 6 January 1066. That was remarkably rapid (Edward had waited for months to be crowned). Everything about the way Harold became king shows him seizing his opportunity.

The Witan

In Anglo-Saxon England, a king's eldest child did not automatically become king when the old king died. Instead, the Witan met to agree who should be king. Often the choice of successor was obvious, but not always. The Witan would be influenced by the needs of the kingdom. Sometimes military strength was more important than being closely related to the dead king.

Because Edward died just after Christmas, and just after the consecration (blessing) of his huge new cathedral in Westminster, a large number of the Witan was already gathered at Edward's palace. Edward died on 5 January and the Witan met on the same day to elect Harold as king. Certainly, the Witan suspected that William would act on his claim to the throne (possibly with Tostig as his ally) and it was probably the need to make preparations for England's defence that made the Witan willing to elect King Harold II as quickly as possible. When news of the coronation reached William, he reacted furiously.

King Harold's challenges

An Anglo-Saxon king only remained in power if he could hold off the challenges of others. Harold faced significant challenges both within England and from outside his realm.

- Challenges from other powerful Anglo-Saxon earls: especially Wessex's old rival, Mercia.
- Acceptance in the north: would Northumbria accept Tostig's brother as king?
- Tostig: Harold's brother was travelling around Europe looking for allies against Harold, as their father, Godwin, had done against King Edward.
- William of Normandy: reports that William was building an invasion fleet soon reached the king.

King Harold's responses

- Straight after his coronation, Harold went to York, the chief city of Northumbria. This was to meet with Witan members who had not been present in London, and ensure he had their support. It was politically vital that the north did not choose this moment to cause problems.
- He then gathered the largest army England had ever seen. This army was positioned along the south coast of England to defend against invasion. He also stationed a large fleet on the south coast. Both the army and the fleet were levied (raised) from the fyrd.

Tostig gained support in Flanders (he was married to Count Baldwin of Flanders' sister). From Flanders, Tostig sailed a fleet over to England in May 1066. But when he learned about the extraordinary strength of Harold's defences, Tostig left quickly and sailed round the coast to Lincoln, where a fight with the Mercians left Tostig with only 12 ships. He fled Lincolnshire too, for Scotland, and began plotting with Harald Hardrada instead.

Harold's army and fleet guarded the southern coast all summer. Tostig's arrival in May might have triggered these defences earlier than planned. Harold had to keep his army and fleet provisioned: an expensive and complicated business. But the expected Norman invasion did not come. By September, it was time to stand down the army and refit the fleet.

1.3 The rival claimants for the throne

The battles of Gate Fulford and Stamford Bridge

Timeline
Gate Fulford and Stamford Bridge, 1066

- **8 September** Southern fyrd disbanded
- **19 September** Harold hears of Hardrada and Tostig's invasion
- **20 September** The Battle of Gate Fulford; Harold leaves London
- **25 September** The Battle of Stamford Bridge

As summer ended, in September 1066, Harald Hardrada and Tostig launched their attack. Hardrada's fleet numbered around 200–300 warships, carrying perhaps 10,000 Viking warriors. From the River Humber, they marched up to York, which had been the capital of a Viking state only a generation before. Their way was blocked by an army led by Morcar and his elder brother, Edwin, the earls of Northumbria and Mercia, at a place called Gate Fulford. The brothers had decided on open battle to defend York rather than staying behind the security of the city's heavy fortifications.

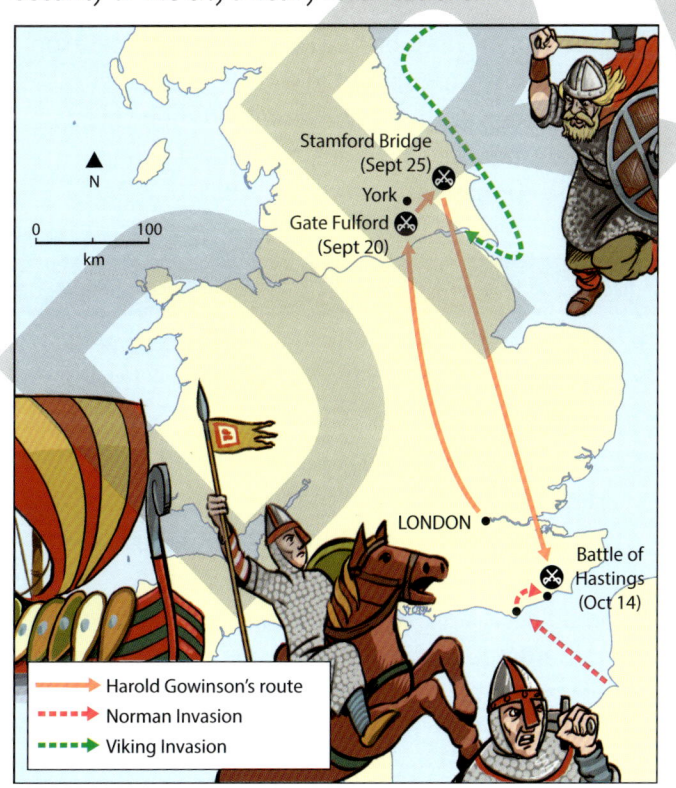

Figure 1.6 Map showing Harold's march north and return south to face invasion of William of Normandy.

Gate Fulford (20 September 1066)

Gate Fulford was a crushing defeat for Edwin and Morcar. There were a number of military reasons for this outcome:

- Edwin and Morcar may have been outnumbered: it is thought they had 6,000 troops against perhaps 9,000 for Hardrada and Tostig (we know some thousands stayed with the ships).
- Hardrada and his housecarls were battle-hardened veterans, and he used a clever strategy in the battle. He positioned Tostig's weaker troops on one wing and, when the English rushed at them, he was able to hit them with his best troops from the side.
- Edwin and Morcar stationed their army with marshland at their backs. This meant their troops had nowhere to go when they were pushed back.

The English army broke and tried to run away into the marsh, but they got stuck in the swampy ground and were cut down. The Norwegians boasted that there were so many dead Englishmen lying in the marsh that they could walk across it without getting their boots muddy.

King Harold's march north

Learning of the invasion (possibly by beacon signals*), Harold took his housecarls north, travelling 185 miles in five days. When he set out, he did not yet know about Gate Fulford.

Key term

Beacon signals*

Fires lit along a chain of high places (cliffs, hill tops) to signal over long distances that an invasion had occurred.

Extend your knowledge

'Marching' north?

The Anglo-Saxon thegns fought on foot, but they travelled to battles on horseback; it is also possible that Harold sailed north, as we know he did take his fleet round the southern coast to London. He would not have taken his southern army with him, however. Harold had already given the order to send the soldiers home – possibly just days before learning of the northern invasion. Harold sent messengers ahead to levy a new army as he travelled, probably most of the troops coming from Essex, East Anglia and some remnants of Edwin and Morcar's troops from Mercia.

31

1.3 The rival claimants for the throne

Leaving the southern coast was a terrible decision for Harold. However, at the time, Harold must have been confident that it was now too late in the year for William to cross the Channel.

- The first of the September storms had wrecked some of Harold's own fleet and possibly also drove William back from an initial invasion attempt.
- The wind was still blowing from the north when Harold set off, which he knew would prevent William from crossing the Channel.
- Just as Harold had struggled to provision his army, he knew William would have found it difficult to keep his army waiting through the summer.

Harold's five-day forced march north is an outstanding military achievement. It was very difficult to gather thousands of men and bring them all together in such a short time, and what Harold then did with them was a strategic masterstroke.

After the Battle of Gate Fulford, Hardrada and Tostig had exchanged hostages with the city of York, which had surrendered to them without a fight. They had also demanded many more hostages from all over Yorkshire. Hostages assured good faith on both sides of an agreement, as they tended to suffer if an agreement was broken. Hardrada and Tostig were informed that the extra hostages would be handed over to them at a place called Stamford Bridge. On 25 September, they were at Stamford Bridge, awaiting their hostages, when Harold launched a surprise attack.

Stamford Bridge (25 September 1066)

King Harold had probably learned of the hostage deal as he travelled towards York, and decided on his strategy. There was a small hill overlooking Stamford Bridge, which meant that his army could approach undetected. The battle was a complete success for Harold: Hardrada and Tostig were both killed, probably with many thousands of their men. It is reported that only 24 of Hardrada's longships returned, out of the 200 or more that had sailed in August.

Harold's victory was aided by several military factors:

- The Viking army had their weapons and shields with them, but had left their armour on their ships (it was a hot day) as well as perhaps a third of their men.
- Harold succeeded in taking Hardrada and Tostig by surprise; they probably did not know he was even in the area.
- Hardrada's army had fought a battle five days before and were not expecting to fight another.
- The Viking troops felt misled: they had been informed that England hated its new king.
- Harold's housecarls eventually broke the Viking shield wall*. This shows that Harold's men had great endurance as well as formidable battle skills.

Harold had triumphed and secured his kingdom against a very significant threat. However, news soon reached him (by 1 October) that William of Normandy had landed on the south coast after all, on 28 September. Harold set off south to fight the third and most significant battle of 1066.

Key term

Shield wall*

A military tactic used by both Viking and Anglo-Saxon armies. Troops were set out in a line, several men deep. The men at the front overlapped their shields, with their spears sticking out, to create a strong defensive formation.

Activity

1. As a class, recreate a shield wall. PE equipment works well for this. Is it a good defence? How might you break it?
2. List your top three reasons why Harold beat Hardrada and Tostig at Stamford Bridge. Compare your choices with a partner: do you agree? Have you changed your mind?
3. Imagine you are Harold, deciding how to respond to Hardrada and Tostig's invasion after a summer of waiting for William to invade (and before you've learned of Gate Fulford). Draw up a pros and cons list for staying put in Wessex.

1.3 The rival claimants for the throne

Were the battles significant?

The consequences of both battles were very significant for the following Battle of Hastings. But, there are other factors to consider as well.

Significant because…	However…
Hardrada and Tostig's invasion meant that Harold was not in place to prevent William's invasion.	Harold had already disbanded the southern fyrd in September anyway, as its time was up.
Edwin and Morcar made strategic errors that meant the loss of thousands of men at Gate Fulford (they could have tried staying inside the city walls of York).	Harold was already on his way north before Gate Fulford had been fought. This suggests he didn't think Edwin and Morcar would stop Tostig and Hardrada without his help.
Edwin and Morcar survived Gate Fulford, but it seems they were then unable (or unwilling) to fight with Harold at Hastings. This weakened Harold's army.	This conclusion comes from the fact that Edwin and Morcar aren't mentioned in the sources on the Battle of Hastings: not very strong evidence.
Harold's march south again must have made his remaining housecarls less battle-ready than William's knights.	Harold and his housecarls had just won a victory against the famed Harald Hardrada. Morale must have been high.
Harold's success at taking Hardrada by surprise might have made him over-confident. Instead of waiting for William in fortified London, he rushed to do battle, with fatal consequences.	Harold and the Witan had been waiting and preparing for William for months, perhaps years. A battle on the south coast, on Harold's home turf, may have seemed the best chance of victory.

Activity ?

Concept maps (spider diagrams) are ideal for working out the links between factors and between topics. You can build up a concept map of a topic in three main stages:

a Put your topic (or issue or question) in the middle of a big piece of paper.
b Draw out 'branches' from the central topic to important categories of the topic.
c From those, draw out 'sub-branches' to individual facts or ideas that connect to them.

It is a good idea to colour-code your different categories and add images to make your map memorable.

Try putting together a concept map on 'Harold's problems in 1066'.

Summary

- The rival claimants to the English throne: Edgar Aethling, Harold Godwinson, Harald Hardrada, William of Normandy.
- Harold Godwinson acted quickly to claim the throne, with the Witan's support.
- His preparations for the expected Norman invasion were thorough.
- Harald and Tostig's northern invasion was repulsed, but had serious consequences.

Checkpoint

Strengthen

S1 Describe the claim to the throne of each of the rival claimants.
S2 Give three reasons each that explain the outcomes of the Battles of Gate Fulford and Stamford Bridge.

Challenge

C1 In your own words, summarise the significance of the Battle of Stamford Bridge – why it was important.
C2 How do the events of Harold's coronation relate to how legitimate his claim was to the English throne?

How confident do you feel about your answers to these questions? If you're not sure you have answered them well, try the above study skills activity.

1.4 The Norman invasion

Learning outcomes
- Understand the events and composition of the Battle of Hastings.
- Understand the reasons for William's victory.

Timeline
The Norman invasion, 1066

- **27 September** William's fleet sets sail
- **28 September** Normans land on Pevensey Bay
- **2 October** Harold leaves York
- **6 October** Harold in London
- **12 October** Harold leaves London
- **14 October** Battle of Hastings

The Battle of Hastings (14 October 1066)

Although not everything about the Battle of Hastings is clear, some key events are generally agreed.

1. Harold did not achieve surprise
William's scouts informed him about Harold's advance in time for him to leave Hastings and threaten Harold's army as it was gathering together on a wooded hilltop called Caldbec Hill. There was a rush to gain control of the high ground of the battlefield, south of Caldbec Hill, which Harold won, organising his shield wall along a ridge. There was marshland either side of the hill.

2. William sent his foot soldiers in first
The battle lasted eight hours: very long for a medieval battle. William first sent his archers forward, but the English caught the arrows on their shields. Norman foot soldiers then went up the hill towards the shield wall. The heavy axes of the English did a lot of damage. The Norman cavalry then laboured up the hill, but failed to break the wall. The battle started in Harold's favour.

3. William showed his face
Waves of Norman attacks continued throughout the day, with the Anglo-Saxon shield wall standing firm.

At a difficult stage for the Normans, a rumour went round William's army that he had been killed or wounded. William tipped his helmet back to show he was still alive and rallied his troops.

4. Harold's shield wall is worn down
A portion of Harold's army disengaged from the shield wall to chase William's men down the hill. They were cut off at the bottom and slaughtered. The Normans gradually reduced the Saxon forces until the shield wall began to break up and became much less effective against cavalry charges.

5. The last stand
Harold, his brothers Gyrth and Leofwine, their housecarls and the remaining fyrd troops held their position at the top of the hill, probably in rings of men around their standards. But they were now heavily outnumbered and unable to hold off the Norman cavalry charges. Harold and his brothers were killed, and their housecarls fought to the last man while the remaining fyrd tried to flee. William was victorious.

Activity
Go online and find a site featuring the whole Bayeux Tapestry. Pick one scene from the Battle of Hastings that appeals to you and print it onto A4 paper. Add a caption and labels to the image that include the following information:

a. What part of the battle it is showing.
b. Who you think the Normans are and who you think the English are (hint: moustaches).
c. What you can infer from it about what the battle was like.

The composition of the armies
Elite troops: knights and housecarls
Elite troops are the members of an army that have received special training to fight in a particular way, and are equipped with specialist equipment.

1.4 The Norman invasion

William's knights

- **Gonfanon:** a battle pennant used for signalling manoeuvres.
- **Weapons:** lance, also javelin, sword, mace.
- **Horse:** specially bred to be strong enough to carry an armoured knight and trained for battle. William had to bring his war horses (destriers) across the Channel.
- **Advantages:** devastating charge potential, height advantage for the mounted knight to strike downwards in combat.
- **Disadvantages:** Horses vulnerable to attack, advantage of charge lost when charging up hill.
- **Shield:** kite-shaped, to protect left side and leg.
- **Armour:** chain mail. Probably not onesie-style as shown in Tapestry but with flaps to cover legs. Conical helmet with nose-piece.
- **Saddle, stirrups, spurs:** the knights' saddles held them tightly in place on their horse so they could use their arms freely. The stirrups allowed them to stand in the saddle for a powerful lance-thrust; the spurs helped in manoeuvres.
- **Elite skills:** years of training to fight on horseback, special manoeuvres.

Figure 1.6 Features of Norman knights.

Harold's housecarls

- **Weapons:** javelin, long axe (1.3 m haft, big swing), sword. The housecarls were trained to wield their axes with such force that a well-directed blow could decapitate a horse.
- **Advantages:** a disciplined shield wall was proof against arrows and very hard to break; heavy axes caused severe injuries and took down horses.
- **Disadvantages:** depended on discipline and endurance. Once the shield wall was depleted, its advantages disappeared; opponents could charge through and turn it back to a general chaotic combat.
- **Elite skills:** shield wall, long-handled axe; discipline and endurance. Harold's housecarls were the elite foot soldiers of Europe. Would fight to the death to defend their king.
- **Shields:** usually round, hide-covered wooden shields with central metal boss. Housecarls formed the shield wall, with troops two or three lines thick behind it. Housecarls were practised in making a gap in the wall for axemen behind to strike, then closing the wall again.
- **Armour:** chain mail or metal plates sewn onto leather. Conical helmet with nose-piece. Similar design to Norman armour.

Figure 1.7 Features of Anglo-Saxon housecarls.

1.4 The Norman invasion

Other troops

Both armies had a core of elite troops, but the mass of each army was made up of ordinary soldiers. William had perhaps 800 knights and around 4–6,000 foot soldiers. How many of Harold's housecarls were present is unknown, but he may have had around 6–7,000 men in his army in total. It is likely that the two armies were similar in size, though historians cannot be sure.

William's foot soldiers

These were a mixture of Normans and soldiers-for-hire from all over Europe. Most were probably not trained to fight in co-ordination with the Norman knights. Some of the foot soldiers would have been archers and crossbowmen. Most Norman archers had padded jackets as armour (called gambesons). The others would have been 'heavy' footsoldiers, with chainmail armour, shields and javelins or swords.

Harold's fyrdsmen

Harold's ordinary soldiers were men that he had hastily levied from the fyrd on his trip south. Not all these levies turned up in time and Harold decided to take on William without them. The thegns had good weapons, shields and armour, but the general fyrd may only have had agricultural tools to fight with. There were not many Anglo-Saxon archers – they may have been amongst the troops that Harold decided not to wait for.

> **Exam-style question, Section B**
>
> Describe **two** features of William's troops at the Battle of Hastings. **4 marks**

> **Exam tip**
>
> Make sure you add supporting information to both.

The reasons for William's victory
Tactics

Because Harold lost the Battle of Hastings, it is tempting to argue that it was because he used old-fashioned tactics against the Norman knights. Is this fair? There are arguments in favour of the shield wall:

- Shield wall tactics were sophisticated. At Gate Fulford, for example, Hardrada allowed the English to attack the weak part of his shield wall, his Flemish troops. As they retreated from the English, he turned his Viking troops into the flank (side) of the English and overwhelmed them.
- Shield walls were effective against archers. At first, William's archers made little impression on Harold's army because the shield wall caught the arrows on their shields.
- Early on in the battle, the shield wall also proved effective against the Norman cavalry. Because the horses had to charge up hill, they didn't hit the wall fast enough or hard enough. The housecarls' huge battle axes could chop the horses down.

The fact that the battle lasted all day suggests that both sides were evenly matched. However, while the English all fought in the same way, William had a mix of troops and he could use different attacking tactics until he found what worked.

- At first, his archers made little impression on the shield wall: they had to shoot up hill and stay out of the shield wall's javelin range. But, once the wall was depleted, the archers could get closer and be more effective.
- Cavalry were usually only used against enemy cavalry or to chase down fleeing foot soldiers, but William used them against the shield wall. At first, the tactic didn't work but, once the shield wall had been weakened, the mounted knights could charge through and break it up.

> **Extend your knowledge**
>
> **Norman horsemanship**
>
> Norman commentators were scornful of the English for not fighting on horseback. However:
>
> - The English had in fact invested instead in a strong fleet. This decision came from their long experience of fighting the Vikings, which was based on the fyrd, fortified towns and a fleet to tackle the Viking longships. If the English fleet had been able to engage the Norman invasion force, this strategy might well have paid off.
> - In Normandy, the investment in breeding bigger, stronger horses went alongside long years of training in fighting on horseback. Technological developments were required too: the saddle and stirrups, and also the lance.
> - 'Couching' a lance was a technique for gripping the lance in such a way that the full power of the charging horse went into the tip of the lance. This technique was only just getting established in 1066.

1.4 The Norman invasion

Figure 1.8 A plan of the Battle of Hastings, 1066.

Source A

A scene from the Bayeux Tapestry showing the Anglo-Saxon shield wall facing a Norman cavalry charge.

Activity

1. Describe two strengths and two weaknesses each of William's troops and Harold's troops.
2. Make two points to support an argument that William's tactics were the reason for his victory at the Battle of Hastings.
3. Anglo-Saxon warriors used horses all the time, but not in battle. What reasons can you think of to explain this?

Leadership

It is easy to judge Harold for making mistakes in leadership while William made all the right decisions. In fact, both leaders took enormous risks, although they both made these on the basis of decades of military experience. For William, the risks paid off; for Harold, they did not – but it might easily have been the other way around.

William's leadership

Both leaders faced massive organisational challenges: William to prepare his invasion, and Harold to defend against it. Harold's decision to gather his defences early in the summer of 1066 gave William a major opportunity.

- William's long wait through the summer of 1066 was not just because of bad weather for sailing. William knew that, at some point, Harold would have to disband the fyrd and he was waiting for this news. As soon as this happened, William set sail (and hit the same storm that battered Harold's fleet, which William managed to get through). Waiting shows strong strategic leadership from William.

What weakened the shield wall?

The critical factor in William's victory was therefore the weakening of the shield wall. It is possible that this happened due to a lack of discipline in Harold's army. When Harold's foot soldiers (the general fyrd) broke ranks at the Battle of Hastings, the shield wall began to be badly weakened. It is possible that the English foot soldiers chased retreating Normans because they wanted to grab discarded arms, armour and horses.

It is also possible that the Norman retreat was a tactic called a 'feigned retreat'. Normans had used this before in battles against the French. A body of troops would pretend to flee in panic, hoping that their opponents would lose their discipline and chase after them. It was very risky, because there was a good chance that a pretend flight could turn into a real one. Medieval battles saw really big casualties only when one side ran away, with the other side chasing them and cutting them down.

37

1.4 The Norman invasion

- Keeping his army and fleet together took strong leadership – sources suggest the Norman army gathered at the port of Dives at the start of August. An army takes a lot of feeding and watering – horses as well as men – and William refused to let his soldiers steal food from the surrounding Norman farmers.
- The crossing was also highly ambitious. Transportation of horses in this way had never been done before. The usual process (which the Vikings did, for example) was to find horses in enemy territory as soon as the invaders landed, but the Norman knights could not do this. Their horses were specially bred and trained. Flat-bottomed boats were constructed that horses could be led into. The Bayeux Tapestry depicts this as being a challenging task!
- When William and his troops arrived in Pevensey Bay (a wide bay, ideal for landing from hundreds of ships), he showed strong strategic awareness. The troops marched several miles along the coast to Hastings, where they adapted the Iron Age fort there into a defensible castle. William had organised a 'pre-fabricated' castle to be brought with them from Normandy – prepared in sections that could be put together quickly. This gave his troops some security from attack.
- Once in England, William allowed his men to cause great destruction in the surrounding area. Not only did they take food and drink from the English, and pack horses for transportation, but they laid waste to their surroundings too, burning down houses.

Extend your knowledge

Norman brutality

Some historians think this destruction was a calculated strategy to enrage Harold – this was happening in his home area, after all – to encourage him to come and fight William in open battle. Others would say that the Normans had a reputation throughout Europe for extreme brutality (the 'Harrying of the North' on page 55 is another example) and this was simply their standard way of occupying enemy territory.

Harold's leadership

Harold's military leadership was highly regarded throughout England and it is important not to view the consequences of his decisions out of context. At the time, Harold may have done what he did for very carefully-thought-through reasons. That said:

- Calling out his southern army in May was a problem as he then had to maintain it for four months, before finally disbanding it.

Benefits of Harold staying in London	Justifications for Harold's decision
The sources suggest that Harold waited for perhaps five days in London before continuing down to Hastings. He waited there to gather troops. London was well-fortified and William would have had to lay siege to it. This would have been difficult for an invading army to do, as they also needed to find food and infectious diseases (e.g. dysentery) spread very quickly amongst armies in siege conditions.	<ul><li>If he moved quickly enough, Harold could have bottled William up in Hastings, where he could be starved into submission. Or, Harold might be able to attack William by surprise, as he had done with Hardrada and Tostig.</li><li>If Harold waited in London, there was a good chance that William would get reinforcements from Normandy.</li><li>Anglo-Saxon historians stress that the techniques for defending towns had not developed – Anglo-Saxons were no good at it. William was highly experienced in sieges.</li><li>It is possible that Harold was let down by Edwin and Morcar: perhaps he left without all his troops because the earls of Mercia and Northumbria refused to help him.</li><li>Harold was king of England but Wessex was his home. He had a responsibility to protect his countrymen from Norman pillaging.</li></ul>
Criticisms of Harold's decision	
<ul><li>In getting down to William as soon as possible, Harold weakened his chances of success because he did not have a full levy of men.</li><li>If he was hoping to surprise William, Harold had underestimated his opponent.</li><li>Harold's decision to leave London may have been linked to his outrage at Norman atrocities in Wessex: William may have planned these atrocities so Harold attacked in a rage rather than waiting to be fully prepared.</li></ul>	

1.4 The Norman invasion

- Deciding to rush down to fight William in the south was not Harold's only option. He could have waited for William to come to him, in London.
- If Harold had planned on surprising William, in fact it was the other way around. William learned of Harold's muster point from his scouts and arrived there after a long, early morning march from Hastings, before Harold's army were ready.

Leadership and luck

In the chaos of battle, anything could happen. If Harold was hit in the eye by an arrow, as the Bayeux Tapestry possibly shows, then it was a fate that could as easily have happened to William, regardless of all the strengths of his leadership. For example, the Viking sagas recount that Harald Hardrada was killed by an arrow in the throat at Stamford Bridge. For both Normans and Anglo-Saxons, God's will determined the outcome.

Luck (or God's will) did play a significant role in William's victory, which so easily could have gone in Harold's favour. For example:

- Harald Hardarada's invasion to happen when it did: the consequences of the defeat at Gate Fulford and Harold's rapid transit up to York and down again were to weaken Harold's defences.
- William decided to sail for England after winter storms had begun to make the Channel very dangerous. His fleet was very lucky not to have been destroyed.
- Medieval battles were chaotic – the Bayeux Tapestry shows Odo of Bayeux (William's half-brother), for example, having to rally young Norman knights who were panicking. Despite the differences in tactics and troops, the two sides seem to have been evenly matched (this perhaps explains why the battle went on so long). Despite all his planning and tactics, William was also very lucky not to have lost, and perhaps owes his victory to the indiscipline of the fyrd.

Activity

There's a thinking skills technique called 'Plus – Minus – Interesting' that is a useful tool for analysis and helps with recalling information, too.

a Plus – write a strength or an advantage of the feature you are studying (e.g. Norman troops).

b Minus – write a weakness or limitation of the feature.

c Interesting – write something you find interesting about the feature.

Try this for the topics in this section: it's especially good for comparing troops, tactics and leadership.

Summary

- The Norman invasion was timed to follow Harold's disbanding of the fyrd.
- An attack late in the year was very risky due to storms in the Channel.
- The Battle of Hastings lasted all day, suggesting the two armies were evenly matched.
- William's victory at the Battle of Hastings has many interlinking causes.

Checkpoint

Strengthen

S1 Describe two features of William's troops.

S2 Describe two features of Harold's troops.

S3 Outline the different stages of the Battle of Hastings.

Challenge

C1 Why do you think Harold lost the Battle of Hastings? Give at least three reasons.

C2 Why do you think William won the Battle of Hastings? Give at least three reasons.

C3 'The English lost because their military tactics and strategies were outdated compared to the Normans.' How far would you agree with this statement?

How confident do you feel about your answers to these questions? If you are not sure you have answered them well, try the following activity.

Recap: Anglo-Saxon England and the Norman Conquest, 1060–66

THINKING HISTORICALLY — Cause and Consequence (3a&b)

The might of human agency

1 'Our lack of control.' Work in pairs.

Describe to your partner a situation where things did not work out as you had intended. Then explain how you would have done things differently to make the situation as you would have wanted. Your partner will then tell the group about that situation and whether they think that your alternative actions would have had the desired effect.

2 'The tyranny of failed actions.' Work individually.

The first battle of 1066 was Gate Fulford, when the army of Earls Edwin and Morcar attempted to defend the North against invasion by Harald Hardrada.

- **a** Write down what Morcar's aims were, as Earl of Northumbria.
- **b** Write down what Morcar's actions were.
- **c** Write down what the outcome was.
- **d** In what ways do the outcomes not live up to Morcar's expectations?
- **e** Now imagine that you are Earl Morcar. Write a defence of your actions. Try to think about the things that you would have known about at the time and make sure that you do not use the benefit of hindsight.

3 'Arguments.' Work in groups of between four and six.

In turn, each group member will read out their defence. Other group members suggest ways to reassure the reader that they were not a failure and that, in some ways, what happened was a good outcome.

4 Think about King Harold and Harald Hardrada's invasion attempt.
- **a** Write down what you think King Harold's aims were in September 1066. What actions did he take? What were the consequences?
- **b** In what ways were the consequences of Hardrada's invasion not anticipated by King Harold?
- **c** In what ways did Hardrada's invasion turn out better for King Harold (in the short-term) than he might have expected?

5 Think about Earl Tostig and Hardrada's invasion attempt of September 1066.
- **a** In what ways were the consequences of the invasion attempt not anticipated by Tostig?
- **b** In what ways did Hardrada's invasion attempt turn out worse for Tostig than their intended consequences?

6 To what extent are historical individuals in control of the history they helped to create? Explain your answer with reference to specific historical examples from this topic and others you have studied.

Exam-style question, Section B

Explain why there was a succession crisis after the death of Edward the Confessor.

You may use the following in your answer:
- Normandy
- the Witan

You **must** also use information of your own. **12 marks**

Exam tip

This question is about causation. Six marks are for knowledge and understanding, six are for your analysis skills, so do not just describe what happened after January 1066. You need to identify the features of the succession crisis, then develop evidence to support each point.

Recap: Anglo-Saxon England and the Norman Conquest, 1060–66

Recall quiz

1. Who was the king of England before Harold?
2. Where was Harald Hardrada king of?
3. Name three of Harold Godwinson's brothers.
4. What was a burh?
5. What was the name for a 'free farmer' in Anglo-Saxon England?
6. List the four main claimants to the English throne after Edward died in January 1066.
7. Who won at Gate Fulford?
8. Who won at Stamford Bridge?
9. Name a tactic used by William at the Battle of Hastings.
10. Two of Harold's brothers died with him at the Battle of Hastings. What were their names and where were they earls of?

Source A

An Anglo-Saxon poem about a great English battle against the Vikings, which ended in an English defeat (the Battle of Maldon, 991), has a thegn saying:

I give you my word that I will not retreat
One inch; I shall forge on
And avenge my lord in battle.
Now that he has fallen in the fight
No loyal warrior living [...]
Need reproach me for returning home lordless
In unworthy retreat, for the weapon shall take me,
The iron sword.

Exam-style question, Section B

'The main reason for the English defeat at the Battle of Hastings was superior Norman tactics.'

How far do you agree? Explain your answer.

You may use the following in your answer:
- the feigned retreat
- the shield wall

You **must** also use information of your own. **16 marks**

Exam tip

This is a question about cause. Remember that 'How far do you agree?' always means the need for analysis of points that support the statement and points that support other causes. The information provided to help you should be used in your answer, but remember that not using information of your own limits the number of marks.

Activity

1. Anglo-Saxons wrote epic poetry about bravery in battle and the honour of dying for their lord. Write a poem of your own, expressing the feelings of an Anglo-Saxon thegn who fought with Harold at the Battle of Hastings. Make it as epic as possible.
2. Put together a news-style report on the contenders for the throne of England following Edward's death in January 1066. Role-play interviews with the main contenders (make sure you use appropriate accents – you'll need a Hungarian accent for Edgar).
3. Draw a big concept map (spider diagram) for the topic: Reasons for William's victory. You will need to decide on some categories for your diagram – for example, tactics, luck, leadership, troops. Use A3 paper and colour-code your categories to help make them more memorable.

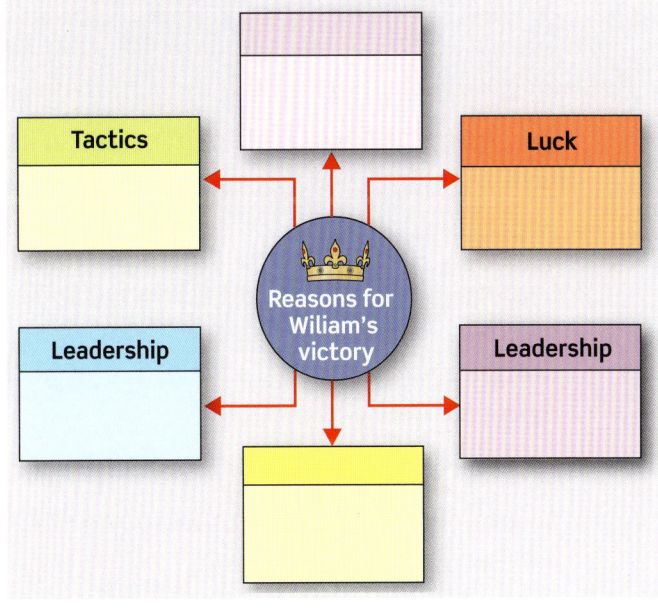

Reasons for William's victory:
- Tactics
- Luck
- Leadership
- Leadership

WRITING HISTORICALLY

Writing historically: managing sentences

The most successful historical writing is clearly expressed, using carefully managed sentence structures.

Learning outcomes

By the end of this lesson, you will understand how to:
- select and use single clause sentences
- select and use multiple clause sentences.

Definitions

Clause: a group of words or unit of meaning that contains a verb and can form part or all of a sentence (for example, 'William I conquered the Anglo-Saxons')

Single clause sentence: a sentence containing just one clause (for example, 'William I conquered the Anglo-Saxons.')

Multiple clause sentence: a sentence containing two or more clauses, often linked with a conjunction, (for example, 'William I conquered the Anglo-Saxons and ruled England for 21 years.')

Coordinating conjunction: a word used to link two clauses of equal importance within a sentence (for example, 'and', 'but', 'so', 'or', etc.)

How can I structure my sentences clearly?

When you are explaining and exploring complex events and ideas, you can end up writing very long sentences. These can make your writing difficult for the reader to follow.

Look at the extract below from a response to this exam-style question:

> Describe **two** features of the social system of Anglo-Saxon England.

> Someone's position in Anglo-Saxon society depended on how much land they owned but the thanes who were the local lords could lose their land and become peasants or slaves and the ceorls who were free farmers could rise to become thanes.

1. The writer of the response above has linked every piece of information in his answer into one, very long sentence.

    How many different pieces of information has the writer included in this answer? Re-write each piece of information as a **single clause sentence**. For example:

    > The thanes were local lords.

2. Look again at your answer to Question 1. Which of the single clause sentences would you link together? Re-write the response twice, experimenting with linking different sentences together using **conjunctions** such as 'and', 'but' or 'so'. Remember: you are aiming to make your writing as clear and precise as possible.

3. Write three two-clause sentences using conjunctions on the topic of the Anglo-Saxon social system.

4. Rewrite the response to the exam-style question, taking into consideration single clause sentences and the use of conjunctions.

WRITING HISTORICALLY

How can I use conjunctions to link my ideas?

There are several types of **multiple clause sentence** structures that you can use to link your ideas.

If you want to balance or contrast two ideas of equal importance within a sentence, you can use coordinating conjunctions to link them.

Look at the extract below from a response to this exam-style question:

> Explain why William was able to become King of England after the Battle of Hastings.

> William's tactics were a key reason for his success. He marched on London and harried and burned the areas through which he passed. This not only intimidated his enemies but also destroyed their capacity for resistance. In the end he took London not through battle but because the earls submitted to him at Berkhamstead and accepted him as king.

These **coordinating conjunctions** link equally important actions that happened at the same time.

These **paired coordinating conjunctions** contrast two possible causes.

These **paired coordinating conjunctions** link and balance two equally important ideas.

5. How else could the writer of the response above have linked, balanced or contrasted these ideas? Experiment with rewriting the response, using different sentence structures and different ways of linking ideas within them.

Did you notice?

The first sentence in the response above is a single clause sentence:

> William's tactics were a key reason for his success.

6. Why do you think the writer chose to give this point additional emphasis by structuring it as a short, single clause sentence? Write a sentence or two explaining your ideas.

Improving an answer

7. Now look at the final paragraph below, which shows a response to the exam-style question above about William becoming king after the Battle of Hastings.

> William's campaigns and tactics had convinced the earls of his military superiority. William had rewarded his followers from the royal treasury seized at Winchester. Edgar's position was growing weaker. Many of the best Anglo-Saxon warriors had been killed at Hastings. The Anglo-Saxons were demoralised. The earls at Berkhamstead submitted. They did not want to face a further campaign they felt they could not win.

Rewrite this paragraph, choosing some conjunctions from the **Coordinating Conjunction Bank** below to link, balance or contrast the writer's ideas.

Coordinating Conjunction Bank	
and	not only… but also…
but	either… or…
or	neither… nor…
so	both… and…

43

Preparing for your exams

Each book has a section dedicated to explaining and exemplifying the new Edexcel GCSE (9-1) History exams. Advice on the demands of every paper, written by **Angela Leonard**, suggests ways students can successfully approach each exam. Each question type is then explained through annotated sample answers at two levels, showing clearly how answers can be improved.

Preparing for your exams

Preparing for your GCSE Paper 2 exam

Paper 2 overview

Your Paper 2 is in two sections that examine the Period Study and British Depth Study. They each count for 20% of your History assessment. The questions on Anglo-Saxon and Norman England are the British Depth Study and are in Section B of the exam paper. You should save just over half the time allowed for Paper 2 to write your answers to Section B. This will give you a few moments for checking your answers at the end.

History Paper 2	Period Study and British Depth Study			Time 1 hour 45 mins
Section A	Period Study	Answer 3 questions	32 marks	50 mins
Section B	Medieval Depth Options B1 or B2	Answer 3 questions	32 marks	55 mins

Medieval Depth Option B1 Anglo-Saxon and Norman England c1060–88

You will answer Question 4, which is in three parts:

(a) Describe two features of... (4 marks)

You are given a few lines to write about each feature. Allow five minutes to write your answer. It is only worth four marks, so keep the answer brief and not try to add more information on extra lines.

(b) Explain why... (12 marks)

This question asks you to explain the reasons why something happened. Allow 20 minutes to write your answer. You are given two stimulus (information) points as prompts to help you. You do not have to use the prompts and you will not lose marks by leaving them out. Always remember to add in a new point of your own as well. Higher marks are gained by adding in a point extra to the prompts. You will be given at least two pages in the answer booklet for your answer. This does not mean you should try to fill all the space. The front page of the exam paper tells you 'there may be more space than you need'. Aim to give at least three explained reasons.

(c)(i) OR (ii) How far do you agree? (16 marks)

This question is worth half your marks for the whole of the Depth Study. Make sure you have kept 30 minutes to answer it. You have a choice of statements: (i) or (ii). Before you decide, be clear what the statement is about: what 'concept' it is about and what topic information you will need to respond to it. You will have prompts to help as for part (b).

The statement can be about the concepts of: cause, significance, consequence, change, continuity, similarity or difference. It is a good idea during revision to practise identifying the concept focus of statements. You could do this with everyday examples and test one another: *the bus was late because it broke down = statement about cause; the bus broke down as a result of poor maintenance = statement about consequence; the bus service has improved recently = statement about change.*

You must make a judgement on **how far you agree** and you should think about **both** sides of the argument. Plan your answer before you begin to write and put your answer points in two columns: For and Against. You should consider at least three points. Think about it as if you were putting weight on each side to decide what your judgement is going to be for the conclusion. That way your whole answer hangs together – it is coherent. Be clear about your reasons (your criteria) for your Judgement – for example why one cause is more important than another? Did it perhaps set others in motion? You must **explain** your answer.

On the one hand
- Point 1

On the other hand
- Point 2
- Point 3

Conclusion

Preparing for your exams

Paper 2, Question 4a

Describe **two** features of towns in Anglo-Saxon England. **(4 marks)**

Exam tip
Keep your answer brief. Two points with some extra information about each of them.

Average answer

Each shire had its main town called a burh which had strong walls. Towns were important for trade.

Identifies two features, but with no supporting information.

Verdict

This is an average answer because two valid features are given, but with no supporting information. Use the feedback to rewrite this answer, making as many improvements as you can.

Strong answer

The main Anglo-Saxon towns were called burhs. Burhs were fortified with strong walls that protected inhabitants from attack by Viking raiders.

Identifies a valid feature and provides supporting information (protection from attack) that is directly related to it.

Towns were important for trade, especially the burhs. In Anglo-Saxon England, all trade worth a certain amount of money had to take place in burhs by law, so that this trade could be taxed.

Again, the valid feature (that towns were important for trade) is supported with information that relates directly to why this was important.

Verdict

This is a strong answer because two valid features are given, with supporting information.

NEW for the 2016 specification

Like what you see in the Student Books?
There's even more available online...

We've created a whole host of time-saving digital tools and materials to help you plan, teach, track and assess the new Edexcel GCSE (9–1) qualification with confidence.

ActiveLearn
Digital Service

- **Editable lesson plans you can tailor to your students**
  - ✓ Linked to the Edexcel schemes of work
  - ✓ Filled with differentiation ideas to engage all your students with history

- **Online Student Books (ActiveBooks) to use with your classes**
  - ✓ Include zoomable sources, images and activities, perfect for front-of-class teaching
  - ✓ Embedded teaching and learning resources to inspire your lessons, such as video introductions and source materials for the Historic Environment unit

- **Ready-made student worksheets**
  - ✓ Designed to complement the Student Books and lesson plans
  - ✓ Editable, so you can personalise them to your students' needs

- **Extra materials for Thinking Historically and Writing Historically**
  - ✓ Teacher notes to help you use the Student Books' *Thinking Historically* and *Writing Historically* pedagogies with your classes
  - ✓ Additional worksheets to support your students as they develop their conceptual understanding and historical literacy skills

- **Assessment materials to help your students get set for the new exams**
  - ✓ Exam skills PowerPoints with exam questions and sample answers
  - ✓ Realistic exam-style assessments and mark schemes for each unit – ideal for exam practice
  - ✓ Diagnostic assessments linked to the Pearson Progression Scale to help you and your students pinpoint strengths and weaknesses

Sign up to hear more at www.pea